Mr. Tingles' Mysteries

The Curious Case of the Bodiless Head

Sean D. Roach

Dedications:

To dad – for believing in and accepting me unconditionally, and encouraging my passion for the mysterious, murder and otherwise.

To Jason – for loving me and *always* making me feel like I'm good enough.

To the Duchess and Lady – for being my friends and accepting me, even when I'm on my soap box (or, *especially* when I'm on my soap box!)

Acknowledgments

I would first like to thank Jason Roach and Gold Dust Publishing for their noble work of uplifting queer voices. Next, I would like to acknowledge our editor, Lynn Picknett, for her thoughtful and constructive insight – your guidance made this a better book and me a better writer. To the author community of which I am so fond – thank you for your acceptance of Jason and I and for expanding our community. I am grateful. To every friend and family member who has touched my life in some way, big or small, thank you. To every mystery writer who has created a captivating story – your work has made this one possible. Finally, I would like to acknowledge the Queer community, of which I am part. Your beauty, creativity, and resilience are magical and I am honored to use my work to represent us in the best way possible.

PROLOGUE

Police cars surrounded 425 South River Street in Reidsville, North Carolina on the 5th of August 2023. The location, The Southern Bank, was a ninety-year-old institution owned by the richest family in the town. The founder, Charles C. Southern, III, had been raised by a housewife and a poor tobacco farmer; with no financial training whatsoever Charles committed himself to doing well in school, going off to college, and rising above his meager upbringing. He was the first in his family to graduate from high school, much less college. His son, grandson, and great-grandson continued his legacy of being highly educated people and pillars of the town's financial industry. None of them, however, could have anticipated the events of August 5th, 2023.

Four bank employees, three clients, two police officers, and twenty-seven onlookers stood in the unbearable

August heat. Police tape surrounded the building where the blinds had been closed on every window to prevent prying eyes from peeking in. A black SUV pulled into the parking lot, slowly making its way through the crowd of small-town investigators. Behind the wheel was the only police detective in town, Isaiah Gentry. Isaiah, like Charles C. Southern, III, was the first in his family to graduate from high school and college. He would have been the pride and joy of his family if he hadn't been outed as a flaming homosexual in his senior year of high school. From that moment forward his father ceased all communication with him and his mother spent their minimal conversations pledging to pray for him. Landing a job as the town's police detective was, though he didn't realize at the time, a feeble attempt to prove to his parents - and perhaps himself - that he was a successful, intelligent man. In fact, he'd only been on the job a year and a half and hadn't yet convinced them he was more than a "faggot." Little did Isaiah know, however, he hadn't been adequately trained for what he was about to see. As he made his way through the small crowd, he recognized a face. "Shit," he thought. "Already?" The face belonged to Kimmie Flague, a local reporter for *The Reidsville Rag*. Kimmie was good at her job because she had no boundaries, no ethics, and nothing else to do. She'd attend the opening of an envelope if she were aware of the event. Isaiah breathed deeply as he prepared to be bombarded by her endless questions and embarrassing attempts to flirt her way to the crime scene.

Isaiah parked the SUV, quickly opening the door, unlatching his seatbelt, and stepping out. He stood 6'3 with dark brown hair combed over to the left and a statuesque build except for his belly - he always gained weight in his belly and ass, and nowhere else. His face was rugged and smooth, and his eyes were hazel and glowed in the sun; he always considered his eyes and his ass his best assets. He started towards the door of the bank and as expected, Kimmie Flague awaited his arrival.

"Detective! Detective Gentry…." she started.

"Kimmie," Isaiah replied flatly. "I don't know anything yet and I have no comment."

"Now, Detective Gentry. You mean to tell me the only police detective in Reidsville - and a very handsome one at that - doesn't have a *single thing* to comment on about what's happenin' here?"

"No comment," Isaiah replied as he stepped through the police barricade and approached the door of the bank, leaving Kimmie frustrated.

As Isaiah stepped inside, he immediately smelled something rancid. He must have worn it on his face because the police officer standing closest asked, "You need a mask, Detective?"

"Got a feeling it won't help," Isaiah responded. "But shit,

yeah give me one." He slid the straps behind his ears and adjusted it over his nose. "What the hell is that?"

"Won't take ya' long to find out," the officer replied, pointing to the small group of police officers and one bank employee.

Isaiah headed towards the group. In a town as small as Reidsville he knew everyone standing there: Officers Carter, Jacobs, and Johnson, and the bank manager, Sheila Flague - Kimmie Flague's sister-in-law. Of course, no sooner than she leaves the bank she'll be on the horn with Kimmie, of that Isaiah could be sure. *The Reidsville Rag* thrived on this type of gossip and one of the primary sources of Kimmie's success was her unparalleled ability to sustain the trust of people who had no reason to trust her. Sheila wasn't a known gossip, to his knowledge, but the family tie was an obvious invitation for her to dish to a concerned party. The officers had all worked under Detective Gentry for his year-and-a-half tenure with the Reidsville Police Department. Carter and Jacobs were in his graduating class and major bullies. They'd tamed a lot in their adulthood but the memories of getting his "faggot ass" kicked persisted. Johnson was the most tenured police officer on the force with forty years on the job. He was well-respected by the community and everyone on the force. He was stubborn, but smart and good at his job.

"Johnson, what do we have?" Isaiah asked, jumping right

in.

"Gentry, I ain't never seen no shit like this in my life. It's in there on the table. Just lift that lid up," Johnson said, seemingly in shock and pointing towards the bank's safe deposit box room.

Detective Isaiah Gentry stepped into the room where the rancid smell immediately evolved into an offensive assault on every sense in his body. "Shit!" he exclaimed. The room was lined with walls of safe deposit boxes of all sizes. Most of the boxes had been forced open. A large table was in the middle of the room and a door gave way to a smaller room with no windows or cameras and another table. On top of the large table was a single safe deposit box; he noted it must be the largest the bank had available - *what the hell is in that thing?* Isaiah, who had forgotten to get gloves before entering the room, pulled a pen out of his pocket and used it to lift the lid of the safe deposit box. As he lifted the lid it became apparent what was inside it. "Ho...ly shit," he said slowly.

There in the center of the box was a severed head. He couldn't tell what gender it might have belonged to but… it was most certainly a head. Besides, if the appearance hadn't convinced him, the smell would have. He stood for several minutes taking in the box, the head, and the room. Johnson still stood behind Isaiah looking away from the room. When Isaiah had seen enough for his own comfort he turned around and approached Johnson, Carter, Jacobs, and Sheila.

"Anywhere we can talk that doesn't smell like…" he started.

"Shit?" Jacobs finished.

"Right," Isaiah said.

"Detective Gentry, we can go to my office," Sheila offered.

"Thank you," Isaiah replied, following Sheila to her office several yards away and motioning for Johnson to follow. Once they arrived Isaiah began questioning Sheila.

"Sheila, you'll understand if we skip pleasantries. Can you tell me what happened?"

"I…." she started. "I started smelling something this morning. Took us some time to figure out where it was coming from, but we narrowed it down to the safe deposit box room. We had to have them drilled open until we found the source and… who knew that's what we'd find." She'd started crying as she was speaking.

"I know it's upsetting, Sheila. I'm sorry you've had to experience this. Can you tell me who the safe deposit box belongs to?"

"I've given the paperwork to officer Johnson," she replied. "She was a young woman, long blonde hair, glasses, about 5'7", athletic build… she was very nice. We talked about gardening, country music, what church she goes to… I just don't understand."

"Did she have anything with her when she came in? Anything large enough to hold a… head?"

"Not at that time. She came in several other times to access the box, though. She always brought in a big bag. Just looked like a purse." Sheila was struggling to speak by this time and Isaiah knew it was time to stop.

"Sheila, we'll take a break for now and finish talking in a little while. Take a seat but do me a favor and don't leave."

Sheila collapsed into her office chair while Johnson and Isaiah walked into the lobby of the bank. Isaiah motioned for Carter and Jacobs and asked them to ensure she was taken care of. He was already overwhelmed by the situation. He hadn't dealt with a murder case on his own yet, and certainly nothing else came close to this. He hardly knew where to start investigating the discovery of a decapitated head. A mile-long to-do list, in no particular order, was developing in his mind as he stood there in the bank's lobby: We need to identify the victim, track down the woman who owns the box, notify the family of the victim, question the other bank employees, finish interviewing Sheila when she gets her shit together, figure out who was in the bank when the woman came in, put together a press release (*not* for Kimmie, for the public), pull camera footage from the bank, bag and tag the evidence… "Jesus," he said aloud.

"I know. It's a fuckin' mess, ain't it?" Johnson asked, having gained some composure from the initial state of shock Isaiah found him in. "Told ya' this wasn't nothin' like what we'd seen 'round here before."

"Yeah, you weren't kidding," Isaiah replied solemnly. "Guess we have no idea who that head belongs to?"

"Naw. No way anyone'd recognize it in that state. Have to get it to the lab for an ID. Already called 'em and they're on the way," Johnson answered.

"Great, thanks. We need to get video footage from the bank on the day this woman came in and every day since and identify the body. Past that I'm at a loss."

"This is a big case for a rookie, Gentry. No offense," Johnson retorted.

"None taken. I'm aware."

"Maybe callin' someone in would help with somethin' like this," Johnson offered. "Only detective in a small town of drunks and addicts - you could use some additional resources."

"Not a bad idea," Isaiah said, considering their options. "But this isn't jurisdiction for the FBI, so I don't know who we could call. Any recommendations?"

"Name Tingles mean anything to you?" Johnson asked.

"Can't say it does," Isaiah answered looking at Johnson with skepticism. *Tingles?*

"Surprising," Johnson shot back, seemingly actually surprised. "He's a… well… he's one of y'all if you get my drift. Thought you might know him."

"We don't all know each other," Isaiah snapped back.

"Alright, alright. I didn't mean no offense. Look, Tingles was a detective and a college professor at the University of North Carolina. Taught criminology. He's worked a ton of high-profile cases and solved all but one or two, I think. He's retired now but still lives in the area. I worked with him on a case here in Reidsville years ago; we didn't solve it, but he's solved hundreds of high-profile cases in the years, before and after. You want somebody who can help solve this case - *that's* your man. Well… not *your man*, but…"

"Shut up, Johnson," Isaiah said, this time smirking. Johnson meant well and Isaiah enjoyed watching him squirm when he thought he was being offensive. "So, we give Mr. Tingles a call. Can't make this shit any worse."

CHAPTER ONE

M r. Tingles was a 64-year-old man who stood 4'11", plump, and, as they say in the south, as sissy as could be. Not only a revered detective, but Mr. Tingles (who had long preferred not to be called "Detective Tingles" because he thought it sounded entirely too manly) was also a staunch advocate of queer rights, women's rights, and all the other rights of minorities that conservatives in a town like Reidsville, North Carolina would sooner die than watch come to fruition. Tingles had marched on Washington for gay rights, volunteered for Act Up during the AIDS epidemic (amid watching hundreds of his friends die), gone door-to-door for Obama *and* Hilary Clinton, and walked in countless Pride parades. He was the shamelessly queer, in-your-face flamboyant, total opposite of Detective Isaiah Gentry. When Tingles' phone rang, he allowed it to ring several times as he looked out over the rolling North Carolina fields that surrounded his home. After a gulp of freshly made lemonade, he swiped to accept the call saying, "Yayus, good day, how can I *help* you?" From the other end he heard, "I'm sorry, ma'am, I may have the wrong number."

"*Whale,* who're ya' tryin' to reach and I'll let you know," Tingles retorted.

"I'm looking for a Detective Tingles."

"Lookie there, you got the right number. But please - call me Mr. Tingles. Detective sounds so… *manly.*"

The man on the other side of the line was Officer Johnson of the Reidsville Police Department who, based on his voice, sounded like he immediately regretted his phone call. Tingles could tell they needed help, and although he'd been retired for nearly a decade, he didn't really need to be convinced. He was intrigued by the case Johnson presented to him. Tingles, now living in Winston-Salem, said "I'll be there quicker'n you can say brunch time!" He lived up to his promise and was there in less than an hour. He arrived in an extravagant vehicle - a solid white 1954 Mercedes SL 300 Gullwing, the likes of which no one in Reidsville (at least in recent years) had ever seen.

As he carefully parked the car and deployed the driver's side wing, the crowd of onlookers - including Kimmie Flague - watched in awe. As Tingles climbed out, he noticed the expressions of the crowd around him and knew immediately he would be bigger news than the head. He was dressed in an off-white fitted suit with a half-cloak to match. The cloak was lined with emerald, green piping and accessorized with emerald, green buttons. His shoes, also emerald, green, matched perfectly in color as if made specifically for the suit which, right on par, was also accessorized with emerald, green buttons, and an emerald, green bowtie perfectly tied. On his head rested an off-white fedora with several peacock feathers sticking out the side and an emerald, green jeweled hat pin holding them in place. Black, square, thick framed glasses rested on his face, behind which his bright blue eyes gazed forward like a man exploring an alternate universe for the first time. As he closed the door on his extravagant car the crowd - and the officers awaiting his arrival - stared confusedly as much as curiously at him.

"What the hell is this, Johnson?" Isaiah asked angrily, looking at Tingles' swaying hips move him across the parking lot towards the police barricade. "Is that?"

"Gentry, I ain't seen the man in thirty years," Johnson said, a slight chuckle in his voice.

"We'll be the laughingstock of the fucking town if that's him. You gotta' be fuckin' kidding me. You mean to tell me *that's* the shrewdest mind of detective work of my generation? I mean, he's so gay he practically *floated* across the parking lot! Johnson, this shit ain't gonna' fly. You tryin' to set me up?" he yelled.

"Gentry, goddamnit, I told you I ain't seen the man in thirty years and I mean it. We got a head layin' in there. *A HEAD!* We got twenty police officers on this whole force and, I don't know if you know it, but *just one* detective. We are goin' to need some help here and this man apparently is the help we need. Maybe at least talk to him. Hell, I'd think if either one of us was defendin' him it'd be you!"

"Fine," he said, transitioning into somewhat of a speech. "We'll give him the courtesy of having a conversation with him and then explain that maybe we didn't need the help after all. Maybe the rest of the town, like me, hasn't heard of this Tingles guy and the most gossip that would emerge is that a flaming homosexual wandered into the town and tried to come to the bank. It'll blow over in a few days after everyone assumes he was either friends or fuckbuddies with me and then no one will ever hear or talk about it again."

Tingles was held up at the barricade by the officers standing watch. He was clearly attempting to get past the barricades while the officers were obviously very skeptical. As Isaiah opened the front door of the bank he caught the end of Tingles' statement:

"Young man, I'm not dressed in four layers of fine silk and velvet for my health. I have been called here to help you find a killuh."

"A killuh!?" He heard Kimmie Flague shout: she sounded like a cartoon character.

"Officer Brown let him through!" Isaiah yelled. Then, turning to a whisper as he approached Officer Brown said, "Do you have any idea how intolerable Kimmie will be with the tiniest bit of information about all this?"

"If you say so, boss," Officer Brown said, still amused by the sight of Mr. Tingles.

"You, young man," Tingles began, "Could really do for some etiquette courses. I know a guy. I'll get you his card."

Before Officer Brown could respond to Tingles, Isaiah began walking him into the bank.

"Tingles, is it?" Isaiah asked, looking him up and down

"Yayus. Leroy H. Tingles, IV. Can you believe there are four men in this world named Leroy *Hubert* Tingles. Ridiculous name, innit? I don't know what my family was thankin' when they named the first one or what they were drankin' when they kept doin' it but that's my name and I'm makin' the most of it. You must be Detective Isaiah Gentry - it's a pleasure to meet you."

"It's uh…" Isaiah started hesitantly, "a pleasure to meet you, too, Mr. Tingles. Come this way and we can talk about why we called."

Mr. Tingles could tell Isaiah was embarrassed by him. He'd lived a long life and his choice to brazenly be himself in every way hadn't only intimidated straight people but other queer people as well. In particular, gay men who tried to fit in with the heteronormative majority were threatened by him. The idea that someone could be boldly queer, confident, intelligent, and successful was too much for some of them. Mr. Tingles recognized the signs, however. The way Gentry looked at him with squinted eyes, his pointed tone, the distance he kept between them as they walked, and how quickly he was ushering Tingles in the bank were indicators he didn't want to be seen with him. He wasn't swayed by Gentry's internal homophobia, though. He'd spent his whole life figuring out how to navigate these types of people.

Isaiah walked Tingles into the bank. As he showed him into the lobby Tingles heard a snort from Sheila's office. He noticed Gentry looking over glaringly at Carter and Jacobs and saw them valiantly attempting to hide their amusement at his appearance. This was already a problem for Gentry, Tingles thought.

"Johnson explained to you that we'd found a…" Isaiah began.

"A decapitated head, yayus. What in tarnation do y'all have goin' on out here? Not enough tobacco to pick?" Tingles replied, chuckling.

"Not real funny to us" Johnson retorted.

"Oh, down boy," Tingles said, continuing to chuckle. "When you've seen as many things like this as me you just don't get as emotional about it anymore. The humor helps me cope, if you will. Now show me this bowling ball and let's get to work."

"Right this way." Isaiah said, releasing a deep, frustrated breath.

"Not many cameras in this place, I see." Tingles commented as they walked. "Two up over the teller's seats and one in the lobby. Have you pulled the footage for the month before whoever the safe deposit box belongs to first came in and every day after?"

"A month before?" Johnson questioned.

"Something like this was planned, officerrrr…." Tingles trailed off expecting Johnson to offer his name.

"Johnson. And why do you think?"

"Officer Johnson!" Tingles exclaimed. "I knew I recognized you. You've put on a little weight and aged some, but you're just as strapping as you were thirty years ago, sir. And because it's a head in a safe deposit box, officer Johnson." Tingles said flatly. His tone suggested what he was saying was common sense and Johnson ought to have known. When he didn't appear to know, Tingles added, somewhat condescendingly, "One does not drop off a human head somewhere they know it will be found unless it's planned. There's just no way. Is there closed-circuit television?"

"None." Isaiah replied. "Small town, low crime rate."

"Hm. Perhaps we can check with neighboring businesses and pull their camera footage. However, our culprit got here, they'll be on camera somewhere."

"Why didn't I think of that?" Isaiah thought out loud.

"Stick with me and you'll learn a lot, kid," Tingles replied airily.

The three walked into the safe deposit box room. Isaiah and Johnson stalled at the door while Tingles dramatically removed his cloak, tossing it over a chair outside the room and boldly_approaching the table where the box with the head lay.

"I assume this is our starlet?" He asked as he neared the box. "Smells dreadful. Worse than a drag queen in summer with no deodorant."

"Christ," Isaiah whispered.

"Looks like this poor thing has been dead for a while - several months, maybe longer. When are you expecting a medical examiner to come?"

"She's on her way. Closest to us is Greensboro and she couldn't get here immediately."

"First thing we do is find out who this is. That'll give us a direction to go. Second thing we do is start working on who brought it. Figure those two things out and we may just find out why. Was there anything else in the box?"

"Just what we see there," Isaiah said. "What do you make of it?"

"You boys got any gloves?" Tingles asked, and then fell silent, focused on something in the box.

Johnson swiftly left and returned with a pair of rubber gloves, handing them to Tingles who removed two large rings, one from each hand, and shoved them into his pockets to slide them on. He reached in the box and lifted the head slowly. The hair attached was matted but clearly long. Tingles, however, didn't seem to care much about the head. His attention was on something different altogether. He stood there staring into the box for what seemed like hours until he placed the head down, removed the gloves, dug his rings out of his pocket and placed them back on his fingers, and turned to face Isaiah and Johnson.

"Boys. There is, in fact, something else in that box."

"What?" the two replied in tandem.

"Our first clue."

A few moments later Mr. Tingles had found his way to an office in the bank and sat on the corner of the desk.

With his cloak thrown back around his shoulders he sat in silence, staring into space, ignoring Johnson and Gentry's stares. Every twenty seconds or so Tingles mumbled, "Hm," or "I wonder." Johnson was tapping his foot impatiently. Finally, after nearly ten minutes of silence - save for Tingles *Hms* and *I wonders* - Isaiah started to speak when Tingles abruptly started:

"Do either of you know what *seemannia nematanthodes* is?" He always spoke loudly and confidently, but after the minutes of silence he took the room by surprise.

"No," Johnson and Isaiah said simultaneously, each sounding confused.

"Otherwise known as *Evita*, it is an exotic looking flower that can be found in some areas of North Carolina."

"Evita?" Johnson asked. "Like the movie with Madonna?"

"Oh, my Patti LuPone!" Tingles exclaimed, seemingly offended. "If LuPone was dead, she'd be rolling over in her grave. I'll send you a copy of the *real* soundtrack. But for now, that's not the point."

"I assume this Evita can be found around here?" Isaiah asked, annoyed and trying to get back on the topic of the head in the building.

"Heavens-to-Betsy, no. Not naturally, anyway. *That* is the point, boys," Tingles began. "You see, I found a recently dead Evita flower petal in the hair of that head. That means that not only is the head a message, but there's a good chance so is the flower."

"The bank manager said the woman who owns the safe deposit box told her she enjoys gardening."

"This means one of two things, gentlemen - either the woman brought the flower in after the head and put it in there *or* wherever that poor person was killed the corpse was exposed to the flower. If that's the case, then the person was killed in another region, or the murderer is local and grows the Evita flower on their property. These are among the first questions we need answered."

"So…" Johnson began, "You mean to tell us you've developed more questions than answers?"

"Sir, an investigation always starts with more questions than answers. If you're not asking questions, you're not *getting* answers."

"Mr. Tingles, with all due respect I think we may be able to handle the investigation from here. Officer Johnson is right - I think we expected you'd be able to steer us in a general direction, but we seem a little more confused now than we did before you arrived."

"Detective Gentry," Mr. Tingles said softly, "I implore you to consider the magnitude of this case. You have a head in a room that was left for you to find. You have a rare flower in the hair - this means your suspect is calculated, sophisticated, clever, and talented. I have caught criminals considered to be the most sophisticated of our generation. If you expect to find this one you need someone experienced."

Mr. Tingles hopped down off the corner of the desk and walked to the door of the office, leaving Johnson and Detective Gentry standing inside. With his back to them he could feel their eyes burning into him. He'd always been underestimated. Often, he was questioned because of his flamboyance ("Someone this fruity can't possibly live up to his reputation"). Other times he was underestimated because of his fashion style. In both cases, he thought, being an old queen was the reason people didn't realize he was the police shark he'd spent his life becoming. Every case he was invited to investigate involved a conversation like the one he was having with Gentry and Johnson. A conversation during which he was required to make a case for himself, to convince local law enforcement they needed him. Over the years he'd stopped trying as hard to convince them. Over 100 criminals that local law enforcement officials couldn't catch had been convicted of their crimes after Tingles investigated and caught them. His work spoke for itself - he didn't need anyone to believe he was capable. This confidence - his sense of self-worth - was why so many people hated Tingles. He'd worked a lifetime for it and wasn't willing to give it up for a *baby gay* who was intimidated by his confidence. He decided to tell Gentry and Johnson what he was thinking. He turned slowly to face them, finding, as he knew, the two staring at him.

"Boys, you're right. You don't need me. If you can't see that you need the help, I won't waste my time trying to convince you. You'd be lucky to have me on this case, but I have spent a lifetime making a name for myself. Whether I investigate with you or not doesn't change that. Good luck."

With that, Tingles turned and began walking away. Before he got halfway across the lobby to the door of the bank he heard Gentry's voice - "Mr. Tingles, may I have a few more words?" Mr. Tingles stopped and slowly turned around to face Isaiah who had followed him out into the lobby. He was standing shyly, seemingly embarrassed. Mr. Tingles looked him up and down waiting to hear what he wanted to say.

"I'm sorry, Mr. Tingles. You're right - we do need your help and your reputation precedes you. Officer Johnson tells me you've solved a lot of cases and been extremely successful. This case is above our experience and resources." A few more moments of silence followed until Isaiah continued: "Will you come back to the station with us to discuss how we move forward?"

"On one condition," Mr. Tingles responded.

"What's that?" Isaiah asked with skepticism.

"You tell that brute in there - Officer Johnson, is it? - that Madonna is *not* Evita." Tingles responded with a smirk.

"Johnson, Mado-"

"Oh, I heard him. *Shit.*" Johnson said from the other room. "Patti LuPone. I know."

CHAPTER TWO

Mr. Tingles had arrived at the Reidsville Police Department in his white 1954 Mercedes SL 300 Gullwing to the same reception by townspeople that he'd received at the bank - pure awe. He was already the talk of the town. *Have you seen that fruity man in the ridiculous car? What's he doing here?* These whispers never deterred Mr. Tingles. Hell, he'd been criticized his entire life. He was born and raised twenty minutes from Reidsville in Eden, North Carolina. A shorter-than-average, flamboyant homosexual in 1960's and 1970's Eden, North Carolina could not fly under the radar of the American South. He was bullied relentlessly, beaten by his own parents, ostracized by their church, and developed self-loathing as early as ten years old. The little old town of Reidsville taunting him at this point in his life was laughable. A southern upbringing for any queer person had the potential to develop one of three types of people -

traumatized, resilient, or both. Mr. Tingles was the latter. His entire life he'd worked to find love and appreciation for himself after being raised by ultra-conservative, Christian parents. Now, in his early sixties, Mr. Tingles understood he'd never forget the trauma he'd experienced, but he also understood that he'd overcome obstacles he'd never have imagined overcoming as a kid and that should be celebrated. He'd also survived two gunshots, a kidnapping in which he was held hostage for forty-five days with minimal food and water, more punches to the face and gut than he could remember, and the death of his long-time partner, Sheldon - he was a resilient man as much as he was a traumatized one.

Tingles now sat in a vacant office waiting for Detective Isaiah Gentry. He wondered when Detective Gentry would "come out" to him. Gentry hadn't done a great job of masking the obvious clues that he's a raging homosexual. The way he draws out the ends of his sentences or the way his hips ever-so-slightly sway when he walks, for example. Tingles understood the desire to want to keep his "gay distance." He was probably fighting for his life, as Tingles had, to prove himself *despite* his queer orientation. Tingles had learned in his life, though, that it wasn't his responsibility to make people disclose their sexuality or gender identity to him. People would do so when they were comfortable. He couldn't help thinking, nevertheless, if he'd just come out it would ease a lot of the tension of their working relationship. Something else he'd learned in his nearly 70 years of life was that closeted men or those who tried to maintain a masculine facade when it doesn't come naturally, resent gay men who wear their sexuality on their sleeves. *Goodness gracious - ain't we two peas in a self-loathing' pod!* Tingles thought. At that time the door opened and Donna, the receptionist, walked in carrying a tray of cookies.

"Hey darlin'," she said sweetly. "I brought in some treats for y'all. Sounds like you've got a big day ahead of you. I'll bring some coffee in shortly."

"Oh, thank you Donna," Tingles replied.

Donna was something of a mother at the police station, and known to be kind, funny, and sharp-witted. She'd worked for the Reidsville Police Department for thirty years and knew all the officers. She was protective over them, especially Isaiah. Donna had been a staunch ally of the queer community her entire life. Her mother's gay hairdresser and best friend, Jimmy, spent many evenings in their home as she grew up; the relationship she shared with him humanized a community other people in town would have had her believe were evil or dangerous. She was also the type of woman who fed the hungry, clothed people in need, and had even been known to offer her guest bedroom to people who needed a roof over their heads for a night or two. Indeed, Donna was treasured by most everyone who met her.

"You're welcome, suga'," Donna said. "Be back

shortly with the coffee."

As she left the room Isaiah walked in.

"Starting to think you'd forgotten about lil' ole' me," Tingles said chuckling.

"Sorry, just briefing the rest of my officers on what happened today." Isaiah replied. "I have Johnson finishing up questioning Sheila Flague. Another officer is questioning one of the bank employees who worked directly with the person who bought the safe deposit box. Say the name she gave was Amanda Bloom."

"Bloom, huh? She *really* likes flowers, doesn't she? That's gotta' mean something."

"Are you sure that's not just her name?"

"As sure as I am brown belts don't go with black shoes, young man," Tingles retorted condescendingly, looking at Gentry's waist and footwear. "What's the address this woman gave to the bank? I say we start there."

"Well, if you don't think we have her real name what good will that do?"

"So far everything she's said and done has a meaning. Nothing can be taken at face value. The head - she knew it'd start stinking eventually - intentional. The flower petal I believe is intentional. The last name Bloom, especially considering the flower petal - intentional. It follows that the address she gave us will have some meaning. So, let's see if I'm right and pay it a visit."

"Alright," Gentry responded, opening his case file. "It's 325 Richmond Drive right here in Reidsville."

"Hm. Sounds vaguely familiar. Let's go check it out, detective."

"We're taking *my car*," Isaiah said. As Tingles began to object, he cut him off - "*My. Car.* Matter of fact - as long as you're here, we're always taking my car."

They grabbed their things and headed out as Tingles tried to make a case for taking his car. Moments later Donna arrived in the empty room with the coffee she'd promised.

"Guess nobody wants coffee," she said.

As the two approached 325 Richmond Dr. in Isaiah's black SUV, Tingles became more and more quiet. He had been observing his surroundings as if he recognized them. Isaiah had no idea Tingles had grown up twenty minutes away, much less that Tingles had investigated cases right in Reidsville throughout his career. Nonetheless, Tingles couldn't put his finger on why the neighborhood they'd ventured into looked *so familiar* to him. He had the feeling his heart was in his stomach with every turn.

"Here it is." Isaiah broke the silence parking the car on the street in front of a large home.

Mr. Tingles slowly exited the vehicle. Once his feet were firmly planted on the ground he stared up at the big house. The home appeared to have been built in the 1940's. It was a three-story, twenty-bedroom, white home with a wrap-around porch and tall, wide columns holding up the awning all around. It looked rather boxy, a typical style for the time but not one Tingles found particularly attractive. Interestingly, as soon as he looked at the tall, wide, double doors that, seemingly, gave way to the entrance of the home, he knew why he recognized it.

"Paul DeCordts," he said quietly.

"Who?" Isaiah asked.

"We have been led to this home," he said, turning his head to face Isaiah.

"Why do you think so?"

"The man who lives in this house was the primary suspect in an investigation I conducted in the late eighties and early nineties. I was a young detective in my thirties and Paul DeCordts was as guilty of murdering his business partner as Judy Garland was of being the greatest voice of my generation. We just couldn't find the evidence we needed to get him convicted. It was one of three cases I didn't solve in my career. I *knew* the address sounded familiar."

"But how could this woman have known you'd be here? It doesn't make sense."

"Detective – I think that head was *meant for me*. I know it sounds like a stretch, but something extravagant would need to be done for you to call me. Whoever this woman is knows that. So, she took the time to bring a head to the bank, knowing it would start stinking, and knowing that the new, inexperienced police detective – of which there is only one in the town – would need help. But for it to be *me* that you called it would have to be something big, hence the head. Now to figure out *why me*, and what the flower means. Come now. Let's see who's home."

Tingles started sashaying up the walkway to the front door as Isaiah stood in place for a few seconds watching. Tingles was either putting together the pieces of their case or jumping to conclusions; he admittedly wasn't convinced of one over the other and could tell Isaiah wasn't either. Regardless, he'd made more progress in a few hours than Isaiah had made all day. Isaiah started walking behind Tingles: because of his long legs (compared to Tingles' very short ones) it didn't take him long to catch up. Tingles could tell by how close Isaiah had gotten to him, and the way he kept trying to edge around him on the narrow walkway that he hated walking slower than his natural stride. Isaiah took his place on the porch next to Mr. Tingles who had pushed in the doorbell no sooner than he landed on the surface. They both waited silently, impatiently, Gentry checking his phone.

"Johnson text. We didn't get anything more from Sheila. Nothing useful anyway."

"Our killer won't make this easy on us," Tingles

replied, reaching for the doorbell again.

After another ring of the bell, they heard footsteps approaching. When the door opened slowly a woman, who appeared to be in her seventies, emerged. She was tall, thin, obviously well-to-do and well-dressed. She wore two strands of white pearls around her neck, a long-sleeved fitted shirt tucked into a knee-length pencil skirt with a belt wrapped around her thin waist to hide the tuck – all shades of gray except the black belt. She wore black pantyhose and black flats. Her hair was gray and wound into a tight bun on top of her head, putting her aging, albeit beautiful face, on full display; tucked into the bun was a bright Evita flower. Her eyes were piercing green, staring through a pair of spectacles at the two of them. After examining them for a few seconds she spoke.

"May I help you?" Her voice was rough – she was obviously a smoker, Tingles thought. He recognized her. Could she be….?

"Yes ma'am, thank you," Tingles spoke. "We are detectives and would like to have a word with you regarding an active investigation. May we come in?"

"Do you have identification?" the woman asked. Isaiah removed his badge and showed her.

"Mr. Tingles," Isaiah started, gesturing to Tingles, "is consulting on this case. While he doesn't have a badge, I can vouch for his presence and stature with law enforcement."

"Tingles?" The woman asked, her eyes darting to Mr. Tingles. "*The* Mr. Tingles?" Her voice had raised slightly.

"Yes ma'am," Tingles responded, feeling nervous. Usually, he'd be thrilled to be recognized, but this time was different. He was right – it was Cheryl DeCordts. Neither of them had recognized one another immediately. Tingles wasn't necessarily shocked Cheryl didn't recognize him earlier. After all, it had been over thirty years since she'd seen him and at that time he wasn't nearly as obviously queer as he'd become later in life.

"You've got a lot of nerve showing up on my door," Mrs. DeCordts said. Her voice was still slightly raised but calmer than either of the detectives would have expected given the circumstances. "I'm sorry, gentlemen, I'm going to have to ask you to leave."

"I'm sorry, ma'am, it doesn't work like that. We're here on official police business and your cooperation is not an option." Gentry said, more forcefully than Tingles thought he was capable of. "Now, we don't have to come in if you don't want us to but at the very least, you'll have to speak with us out here. Given the nature of this discussion I'd strongly recommend you let us inside."

The three stood in silence for several moments while Mrs. DeCordts' expression turned cold. Tingles noted she was sizing them up, seemingly trying to calculate her next move.

"Fine," the woman said, though cynically. "You may come in." She let them pass, glaring at Mr. Tingles as he made his way by her.

The woman pointed the two detectives into the sitting room. Antiques surrounded them. Tingles recognized expensive furniture when he saw it and he could tell he was saturated in thousands of dollars' worth of mahogany tables and chairs, silk curtains, genuine classic art, and throw pillows that cost more than his first home. Mrs. DeCordts had offered them a place to sit and beverages that they'd declined. She sat now on the edge of an antique chair, her legs bent back at the knee and crossed at the ankles, her hands clasped and resting on her knee, and her head tilted slightly as to ask, "What the fuck do you want?"

"So, detectives," she said instead. "How may I help you?"

"Uh, well…" Isaiah started. "First, may I ask – are you Mrs. Cheryl DeCordts?"

"In the flesh," Cheryl responded flatly. "But I've a feeling you already knew that."

"Okay. Um… well, do you have a safe deposit box at the Southern Bank here in town?"

"Not exactly," she answered. "My husband had one that I never closed. I assume it's still there, but… I've never asked to access it."

"Why is that?" Tingles interjected.

"Never found a need to. I know what's there," she replied.

"And you don't have one that you bought recently?"

"No, detective, I do not. May I ask what this is about?" Mrs. DeCordts was obviously restless and aggravated by the detectives' questions. Tingles recalled she was a woman who valued directness and wanted people to get to the point. Beating around the bush was a waste of everyone's time.

"Madam…" Tingles began. "You might be surprised to know a young woman bought a safe deposit box at the Southern Bank several weeks ago and put down this address as her own. Today, a decapitated head was found in that box and we're trying to figure out who the woman that bought that box is. Do you understand?"

"I have no idea what you're talking about!" Mrs. DeCordts protested. She seemed offended. "I have certainly not bought a safe deposit box and left a head inside."

"We know," Tingles said, chuckling softly. "I said a *young* woman bought a safe deposit box. Respectfully, Mrs. DeCordts, you are lovely but not young. We need to know who the woman that did buy it is, though. Anyone staying here with you in this house?"

"No – no one is staying in the house, and no one is authorized to use this address."

"Mrs. DeCordts," Isaiah said. "Is your husband

here?"

"In a manner of speaking," Cheryl replied. "He's buried in the family cemetery on the property."

"When did he die?" Tingles asked, genuinely interested in when one of his three mortal enemies had died.

"Last year," Cheryl answered sharply. Mr. Tingles could sense her rising irritation with his presence.

"I'm sorry for your loss," Isaiah said. "I hope it wasn't a hard passing."

"He was a miserable man. Accused of murder years ago and his reputation never recovered," Cheryl responded, turning her cold gaze to Mr. Tingles. "His law practice nearly crashed, lost most of his friends, and then became ill with cancer. *Life* was hard, not his death. It was time for him to go."

"I'm sorry," Detective Gentry said softly. Mr. Tingles cut his eyes at Isaiah and could tell he also was in disbelief she'd offered up the information they already knew about his previous run-in with the law. "Do you have *any* idea, Mrs. DeCordts, who could have used this address?"

"As I said – no one else lives here and no one has permission to use this address except for me."

"Thank you for your time, Mrs. DeCordts," Tingles said, rising. "Detective Gentry, I don't think we need anything else here."

Tingles rose and headed towards the door, Gentry

close behind him. He stopped suddenly and turned back towards Mrs. DeCordts, tapping his chin.

"Silly me," Tingles began, "I do have another question. I notice you have an Evita flower in your hair... we found one at the crime scene as well."

"Is that a question?" Mrs. DeCordts asked, after a few moments of silence.

"No, I don't guess it is," Tingles said.

"Careful, Tingles!" Mrs. DeCordts retorted. "I'd hate to think you came here to accuse *me* of murder."

"I wouldn't dream of it, Cheryl," Tingles said.

The two told Mrs. DeCordts they'd see themselves out. As they passed through the front doors, shutting them quietly behind them and making their way back down the long walkway to the street, Tingles' urge to blurt out what was on his mind nearly got the better of him. As soon as they landed in the car, he erupted.

"She knows something. Why did she tell us about her husband's accusation of murder? Why would she tell us that specifically? And did you see the plant in the entryway? With the red flowers on it – *that's* the Evita. Then the one in her hair? Coincidence? I think not, Detective."

"Wait, wait, wait," Isaiah said. "You don't think that old lady is our murderer, do you?"

"Heavens to Betsy, no!" Tingles exclaimed. "But she's tied to it somehow. She's well past her prime, Bette

Davis in *The Letter* days. But I do think she knows more than she's telling us. Who is she protecting?"

"I have no idea who Bette Davis is, but… A kid maybe? If it's a young woman we're looking for, it could be a daughter. Or hell, a granddaughter, even."

"She only has sons, so maybe a granddaughter is right," Tingles pondered aloud. "Maybe Johnson can find out if she has any. Meanwhile, I'm going to review my case notes from the Darren Southern murder case to see if there's anything useful for us."

Tingles paused and then added:

"And good lord, boy! Bette Davis is a gay icon! *Whatever Happened to Baby Jane? All About Eve.*"

Gentry looked confused.

"We need to broaden your horizons."

Tingles realized he'd inadvertently told Isaiah, "I know you're gay and you're safe with me." He'd still wait patiently for Isaiah to tell him.

CHAPTER THREE

Mr. Tingles settled into his room at the Reidsville Inn. The place was as shabby as he would expect given the size and economy of the town. His own home in Winston Salem was nearly an hour away, and at his age, he didn't feel comfortable driving the distance in the darkness of early morning or evening. He'd convinced Detective Gentry the Reidsville Police Department should pay for his boarding while he was in town. Gentry conceded quickly and easily. Mr. Tingles had packed one overnight bag just in case he got stuck in Reidsville; once he realized he'd be there awhile, he sent for his things and reserved a room at the rinky-dink inn. The carpet was brown, burgundy, and forest green with burn marks scattered across the room. The curtains were solid burgundy and came complete with moth holes to match the carpet. The bed was lumpy, the pillows too soft, the closet too small, the bathroom too dirty, and the television set too fuzzy. However, there was a small desk nudged up to the wall next to the bed and a lamp that worked – that's all Tingles needed.

Johnson had confirmed Mrs. DeCordts had no grandchildren, further confusing the possibility of narrowing down who she was protecting. Tingles couldn't shake the idea the DeCordts_had something to do with this case. That their current murderer used Mrs. DeCordts address at the bank couldn't be a coincidence. He opened his laptop and navigated to his old case files. Several years prior he'd had all of his case files digitized so he could start writing a book about his life. He'd written several books about various cases but never included any of the ones he hadn't solved. Hell, there were only three – why did he need to include them? The time had come, though, for him to face one of his demons – Paul DeCordts. Tingles knew if he was going to solve the murder at hand, he'd have to examine the murder of Darren M. Southern closer. He cringed a little looking at his notes from thirty-five years ago. Experience had made everything about doing his job better – including his notetaking.

November 17th, 1989 – Initial Notes
Victim: Darren M. Southern
Age: 34
Race: White
Cause of death: Single gunshot wound between

the eyes

Profession: Attorney

Spouse: Clara Southern, 30

Children: Shelly Southern, 3

- Victim found in his home by wife around 11:30pm Medical examiner determined he'd been dead at least 2 hours putting time of death between 9:30pm and 10:30pm on November 16th, 1989.
- No forced entry, no weapon found.
- Nothing seemed out of place in the residence. The scene was neat – almost too neat.
- Darren Southern is of the Southern Bank lineage – crime related to money?
- Closest people to Mr. Southern outside of wife and daughter are his business partner, Paul DeCordts, his secretary, Mrs. Dana Frye, and a paralegal at the firm named Devin Anderson.
- Initial interviews with family, Mr. DeCordts, Mrs. Frye, and Mr. Anderson yielded little useful information.
- Darren and Paul reportedly had an argument the day of his murder, but according to Dana Frye this was typical and no cause for alarm.

- Mrs. Southern discovered the body of her husband when she came home from a charity gala. She found her daughter, Shelly, hiding in a closet. Charity Gala is a verified alibi. Shelly was unable to provide any information about the murderer.

November 18th, 1989

- Mrs. Cheryl DeCordts interviewed at 9:27am. States she was with Mr. DeCordts during the estimated time of the murder – she seems to be hiding something.
- DeCordts' have 2 sons: Brent DeCordts and Joseph DeCordts, twins, 12.
- Brent & Joseph interviewed. Their recollections of the evening of November 16th are nearly identical, which is alarming. Details don't vary at all, like it's been rehearsed.
- Mrs. and Mr. DeCordts' recollections of that evening are also very similar to their kids'.
- Something alarming about the cohesiveness of this family's memory…

As he read through his notes Mr. Tingles felt like he was back in those interview rooms listening to the DeCordts family tell him the same story over and over. He felt the same cynicism he did over thirty years ago as he was reminded how similar the four stories were:

- Mr. DeCordts arrived home around 6:30pm.
- Mrs. DeCordts escorted her husband from the door to the sitting room where the children were.
- The family sat together talking about their day until 7pm when Shana, the cook, announced that dinner was ready.
- The family ate dinner together from approximately 7pm to 8pm.
- After dinner, the twins bathed and changed into their pajamas, after which the entire family watched television together until approximately 10pm.
- Everyone went to bed around 10:15pm.
- Mrs. DeCordts rose around midnight and went to the kitchen for water. Brent, Joseph, and Paul all reported hearing her move around the house.

Tingles couldn't fathom four stories as consistent as the ones he'd heard from the DeCordts family which is why Mr. DeCordts was his primary suspect. Now, over thirty years later, he was faced with the task of finding what he'd missed back then and figuring out what it had to do with a head in a safe deposit box with a rare flower in its hair. Tingles knew there were two things that had to happen before he'd have a single clue about who their murderer could be: identify the first victim and question everyone involved in the Southern murder that they could find. It'd been thirty-five years, after all – some of them were dead, to be sure.

There was a part of Tingles that wanted to leave the Southern case in the past. He'd lost more sleep over never finding Darren's murderer than he'd like to admit. It was the first case he investigated that he hadn't solved, and every murderer or criminal he caught he thought to himself, "Could I have done more to find Darren Southern's murderer?" In his retirement, he thought of the case often but had finally come to a point in his life where he'd accepted there were three murderers he just couldn't catch. Whoever murdered Darren Southern was one of them and accepting that was the only way Tingles figured he could die peacefully when the time came. It was just that he'd felt a deep sense of responsibility as a detective to find criminals and hold them accountable. There were too many people in the world not being held accountable for their crimes – if Tingles could help it, none of them would be associated with cases he investigated. That sense of responsibility came creeping back in as he reviewed his notes from the Southern murder case. With what he thought were new clues in the palms of his hands he saw a final opportunity to close the case. He would see it through.

CHAPTER FOUR

Kimmie Flague stood outside the Reidsville Police Department smoking a Marlboro menthol. Two days had passed since the head was found in a safe deposit box in The Southern Bank and she hadn't been able to get a single officer or detective (of which there was only one, of course) to talk to her. Even her sister-in-law was tight-lipped about any of the details, and Kimmie knew, beyond the shadow of doubt, that Detective Gentry had instructed her to do so. Kimmie was determined to find out more about what was going on with the investigation. This was the perfect type of story for *The Reidsville Rag,* and she wanted to be the first to have the scoop. Eventually, bigger publications and the news channels would get their claws in it, but Kimmie knew if she could break the story, it would open doors for her to get the hell out of Reidsville and write for a real publication.

Kimmie had grown up in Reidsville. Her father was the owner of, and a writer for, *The Reidsville Rag* and currently her boss. She'd spent her entire life trying to live up to his expectations. When they got word there was something happening at The Southern Bank, Kimmie was deployed. That meant her father thought it was nothing. Like the rest of the town, he thought all she was capable of writing was town gossip, but she had bigger goals than telling stories about who was cheating on who or who'd been arrested for possession of cocaine. Kimmie was determined to prove her father wrong. Her mother died when she was a child, and she barely remembered her so the only significant person she felt determined to prove anything to was her overbearing father.

As she took a final drag of her Marlboro, Kimmie found a determination to get someone on the police force to provide her with information about whatever happened at The Southern Bank. If she was going to become a real-life Gale Weathers, after all, she was going to have to get her hands dirty. She tossed the butt of her cigarette on the ground, the last bit of the cherry billowing smoke. Kimmie walked confidently away from the cigarette butt towards the police department. As she emerged through the door Donna, who Kimmie knew as well as the officers, grimaced. She *hated* Kimmie; if she'd said it once, she'd said a million times - Kimmie only showed up anywhere to stir up trouble.

Kimmie noticed Donna's expression shift as soon as she saw her but was undeterred.

"G'mornin' Donna," she bellowed.

"Good morning, Kimmie," Donna answered flatly. "To what do we owe the pleasure?"

"Is Detective Gentry in? I'd like a word."

"Now Kimmie," Donna started in her motherly tone. "We both know he has a permanent out-of-office notice with your name on it. He's not going to talk about this case with you."

Kimmie wasn't discouraged. She knew if she couldn't even get the department to talk to her, she'd never get any information to help her write the story of her lifetime. Desperate times called for desperate measures, she decided, as she turned away from Donna and headed toward the offices behind her.

"Donna, that ends today. The public has a right to know!" she said over her shoulder, turning around, obviously angry but determined.

Truth be told, she didn't really care about the public's right to know anything. The only thing on her mind was getting a good story to kickstart her career. As she swung open the door to the offices, she heard Donna protesting. Just as the door shut behind her, she heard:

"Isaiah, Kimmie is on her way to your office. I tried to stop her."

"Nice try, bitch," Kimmie muttered as she came to a stop realizing she'd never been past those doors and had no idea where to find Detective Gentry. Before she had a moment to think any more about it she heard a familiar voice.

"Kimmie – what can we do for you?"

It was Officer Carter. Kimmie had known him since high school; he'd been the fat, geeky kid who had all of two friends, never dated, and was relentlessly bullied. Kimmie was one of his bullies. She'd heard Carter had a crush on her when they were seniors and made his life miserable. "*Ewwwww. As IF!*" she'd said and spat on his shoes. Carter went off to the police academy after high school, and she went off to college, meaning the two of them didn't see each other for approximately five years. When they both moved back to Reidsville the same year, their reunion was chock-full of resentment. The only curve ball for Kimmie was that Carter had gone off and gotten muscular and hot.

"Oh, um…" Kimmie stuttered. "I… Don't you look good today?" she managed to get out.

Carter shook his head but grinned at the compliment. He hadn't forgotten how awful she'd been to him in high school, but if he was being honest, he was still attracted to her. At approximately five feet and seven inches tall, long brunette hair cascading down her back, vibrant hazel eyes, and an hourglass figure, Kimmie was a goddess to most men.

"What do you want, Kimmie? You're not supposed to be back here."

"Oh yeah," she said, giggling flirtatiously. "I need to

see Isaiah. I really think he owes it to the publi…."

"*Whale, whale, whale…* the town gossip. Whatever can we do for you?"

Kimmie swung around and found all five feet, and two inches of Mr. Tingles standing behind her in a light gray and baby blue plaid suit with a matching hat – another large feather standing erect from its side. *"What a fucking fa…"* she started to think when she heard another familiar voice, robbing her of the chance to respond to Tingles.

"What do you want, Kimmie?" It was Detective Gentry. She took a deep breath and asserted herself.

"Detective Gentry and Dete… or, whoever you are… the public has a right to know what's going on, and I'm here to ask some questions. We pay your salaries, and we want to know what in the hell is happening that has had the bank closed for two days and warrants calling in… whoever he is." The last few words of her monologue trailed off and she knew that it was apparent to Gentry and Mr. Tingles she was nervous.

"Well, my name is Mr. Tingles. I am an esteemed and accomplished detective in the United States, and I was called in to assist with this case. You can Google me, suga."

Gentry was visibly aggravated by Kimmie's presence and with Mr. Tingles for entertaining her.

"Come to my office," Gentry said, to Kimmie's utter surprise. Mr. Tingles was surprised, too, and didn't bother hiding it. A high-shrilled gasp escaped his throat.

"You've got to be kiddin' me…." he began. Gentry held up a hand as he led them to his office.

Kimmie noted that Detective Gentry's office was plain. There were no awards on the walls, photos on his desk, or any decor whatsoever. In the windowless room there sat a desk piled with files, one chair behind and two in front of it. The walls were lined with file cabinets – no one knew they were empty. What could be expected of a detective who'd only been in his role for a year and a half in a town that rarely needed a detective? Gentry took his place in the chair behind the desk and gestured for Kimmie and Mr. Tingles to sit opposite. The three sat in silence for several minutes before Gentry spoke.

"Kimmie, I don't trust you, and I think you know why. I have absolutely no interest in partnering with you and providing you with information on this case. You're manipulative, nosey, unethical, dishonest, and an overall pain in the ass. Ya' have been since high school. One thing you're right about is the public does deserve to know what's going on. Unfortunately, *The Reidsville Rag* is the only goddamn paper in this town, and how most of the people in this town get their news. To that end, I will provide you with information on this case as it develops, and I will *only* share information that will not compromise our investigation. Do you understand me?"

Gentry's tone was fatherly. He meant what he said, and Kimmie knew it. As he spoke, she was transported back to high school. She and Gentry were the same age and went to high school together. In their junior year the two dated for seven months – most of the school year. Over the following summer, the day before their senior year began, Kimmie found out Isaiah was gay when she caught him kissing another classmate, Jimmy Temple. Neither Isaiah nor Jimmy knew they'd been seen, but that evening they both walked into conversations with their parents that would change their lives. It didn't take long to discover that Kimmie was the leak. The following morning as she walked by Isaiah in the hallway, she made it a point to ask him how his night had been. "Anything… interesting happen last night?" she'd asked mockingly. From that moment forward Kimmie Flague was the mortal enemy of Isaiah Gentry. Kimmie breathed in slowly, processing Gentry's comments. Her next words were calculated.

"Isaiah, we're not still holding on to the past, are we? That was a long time ago. We're both adults now and trying to make a living. Whatever is going on here is obviously very big, otherwise you wouldn't be trying to hide it. We could both build careers on this, I'm sure, if we work together. I'm glad you're willing to put aside our differences."

"Listen to me, Kimmie. Listen real good. Our 'differences' will never be put aside. You ruined my life. You robbed me of the opportunity to come out to my parents *safely* and on my own time. That isn't 'differences,' you cunning bitch, it's malice. It's a goddamn shame you're the only reporter to talk to in this town, but here we are. Don't you *ever*, for one second, think this is a partnership. The only thing you're getting out of me is what's *absolutely* necessary for the public to know."

Kimmie felt herself becoming angry. Mr. Tingles sat, seemingly at leisure, staring out into space and unphased by the conversation occurring. There was over a decade of tension between the two coming to a head right in front of him, but Mr. Tingles had stood toe-to-toe with some of the country's most villainous murderers. A little couple's therapy content was nothing to him. Kimmie pulled out a notepad and pen as she began to respond.

"Fine," she said flatly. "So, what *can* you tell me?"

Detective Gentry had given Kimmie what she knew was the *Reader's Digest* version of the case. A body part had been found in the bank, and that's all they knew. It might be a big deal; it might not be. Mr. Tingles had listened and declined to add anything when prompted by Gentry. Mr. Tingles had learned a lot about Gentry in his conversation with Kimmie. He'd officially "come out" to Mr. Tingles, for which he felt honored. He'd also learned Gentry wasn't necessarily the novice Mr. Tingles assumed him to be. Sure, he may be a new detective, but he was a skilled leader and didn't mind asserting himself when it really mattered. Now that Kimmie was gone Mr. Tingles wanted time with Detective Gentry to address a few things. Having sat in silence for several moments after she left, Mr. Tingles got up, closed the office door, and initiated discourse.

"Thank you for your honesty regarding your sexual orientation. You didn't have to share that in front of me, but I appreciate that you did. You might not have noticed that I am also a homosexual." Mr. Tingles grinned but, seeing from his face that a smart-ass retort was brewing, didn't give Gentry an opportunity to respond. "That out of the way, we need to talk about this case."

Mr. Tingles proceeded to tell Isaiah he'd reviewed his notes from the DeCordts case of 1989. He was positive there was a connection between the 1989 murder of Darren M. Southern and the head they discovered in the safe deposit box. He wasn't sure what the connection was, but he knew that to investigate *this* case they would have to investigate *that* case. The address provided, along with the flower in the safe deposit box with the head that matched those in Mrs. DeCordts' home couldn't be a coincidence. Isaiah gave Mr. Tingles the respect of listening without interrupting him. Tingles' words hung in the air for several moments after he concluded his dramatic monologue. He could tell Isaiah believed him. His conviction was convincing, but he hadn't offered any insight on where to begin investigating because he simply wasn't sure yet. When he said as much, Isaiah found it hard to believe he hadn't devised a plan. Again, before he could speak Mr. Tingles picked back up.

"The first thing we should do after reviewing all of my notes together and anything your station still has, I think, is question every single person involved in the DeCordts case. Both families involved, witnesses, everyone we can find that is still alive."

As Tingles concluded again, there was a knock at the door. Donna entered the room with a manilla folder in her hand. As she came through the door, she deduced Tingles and Isaiah were in the middle of a serious conversation and excused herself as quickly as she'd entered. Tingles had plopped himself on the corner of Isaiah's desk and looked at the manilla envelope curiously. Isaiah picked it up and gently opened it. His eyes scanned the page and then quickly widened. Tingles knew whatever Isaiah was looking at was serious and perhaps another key to the puzzle of their case.

"You were dead on about the connection. The head we found… belongs to Brent DeCordts."

"Oh, my Cher!" Tingles gasped. "One of the DeCordts' boys... Talk about *turnin' back time!* Time to pay another visit to the DeCordts family matriarch."

"Oh! Cher, I *believe* I know who she is," Gentry said, smirking.

"Well, thank the gay heavens for *that!*" Tingles exclaimed, smiling back.

CHAPTER FIVE

Mr. Tingles and Detective Isaiah Gentry were back at 325 Richmond Dr. within the hour. Officer Johnson and a crew of officers were sent to Brent DeCordts' home. Tingles and Gentry were set to join them after their interrogation of Mrs. DeCordts. Nothing in Reidsville was too far from anything else so it was no surprise to Tingles when it took them nine minutes to arrive from the station. In those nine minutes, he reflected on their short interaction with Mrs. DeCordts the day before. She'd been brusque and cold. She was hiding something, but he didn't know what — *just like thirty-five years ago.* Further, whatever she was hiding couldn't be connected with murdering her son. She wasn't physically strong enough to murder and decapitate him. The more Tingles considered the case, the more he realized nothing made sense. He couldn't put the pieces of this puzzle together, but he hoped after a more stringent interrogation of Mrs. DeCordts he'd be headed in the right direction.

As they had before, the pair marched up the long walkway, up the stairs, and stood in front of the giant double doors waiting for Mrs. DeCordts after ringing the bell. Tingles felt a sense of *deja-vu* as they waited, but also a sense of vindication. He was convinced Mrs. DeCordts was a pivotal figure in their investigation and could possibly lead them to discovering who'd murdered Darren Southern and her son, Brent. The question was whether she'd cooperate. Mr. Tingles had thought up some important questions in the short ride over and knew they'd put Mrs. DeCordts on the defensive. They didn't have time to waste, though, so he wasn't prepared to put up with Mrs. DeCordts' bullshit.

Cheryl arrived at the door as cold as she had the previous day. Dressed again in an array of grays and blacks, she narrowed her eyes at Mr. Tingles and Detective Gentry, an expression that bade them to explain their presence – immediately. Mr. Tingles recalled he'd seen this expression on her three decades ago. Her sharp eyes were difficult to forget, but particularly when they narrowed on him as they currently had. In 1989, she'd narrowed those vicious eyes on him time and again as Mr. Tingles interrogated her over and over about her husband. Each time the expression screamed indignation, annoyance, and secrecy. After all these years she was still hiding something.

"Detectives," she said, pointedly. It wasn't a question but an observation. "Come in, I guess," she said coldly, stepping aside and gesturing towards the sitting room they'd sat in less than 24 hours prior.

"Thank you for your hospitality, Mrs. DeCordts," Mr. Tingles said as he walked by her. His tone was solemn – he still had the task of telling her the head they'd found in a safe deposit box belonged to her son. "We realize you're a busy woman, so we hope not to take up too much of your time." By the end of his statement, they'd reached the sitting room and were taking their seats.

"How can I help you?" Mrs. DeCordts asked dryly, annoyed. "You're right that I'm a busy woman and I am still failing to see how I may be of assistance in this case you're investigating."

"Mrs. DeCordts…" Detective Gentry started, quickly being interrupted by Mr. Tingles.

"Cheryl – I hope you don't mind if I use your first name? We have some heavy news to share with you. The deceased man we referred to yesterday has been identified as… your son, Brent."

Mr. Tingles' words fell between the three of them like a boulder. The room became dreadfully silent as Mrs. DeCordts processed what Mr. Tingles had just said. She didn't cry, or gasp, or react at all, really. Mr. Tingles took note of her lackluster reaction – not what one would expect from a mother who just learned her son was not only dead, but murdered and decapitated. Tingles noted, too, that he wasn't surprised by her reaction. She was always composed and, just like a southern lady, wouldn't dream of inconveniencing her guests with emotions. Again, Tingles recognized this behavior.

"Mrs. DeCordts?" Gentry asked softly. Tingles knew he wasn't in-the-know. He didn't realize she wouldn't behave the way any normal person would expect a mother to behave under these circumstances.

"Is that all you came to say?" Mrs. DeCordts asked.

"We have some questions for you," Mr. Tingles responded. From the corner of his eye he saw Gentry was looking at him as if to chastise him. Tingles ignored him and pushed forward. "When's the last time you saw your son?"

"I haven't seen or talked to Brent in months," she replied coolly.

"Why?" Tingles shot back. The interrogation had begun.

"The last time he was here he asked for money. I refused to give him any and he stormed out. My phone records will show I called him a number of times in the days after. When I couldn't get in touch with him, I decided to give him space. I thought eventually he would come to his senses. He didn't."

"What did he need money for?" Tingles asked.

"His business was suffering, and he needed a bailout. He asked for fifty-thousand dollars. He'd never have asked his father for money. I don't know why he thought I would give it to him."

"What kind of business was he in?" Tingles inquired.

"He owned an event-planning company he bought from a friend a few years back. The pandemic hurt it like it did many businesses. He's been struggling ever since."

"Other than being in need of money, how did he seem when you saw him?"

"Odd, I guess," Cheryl responded. "He seemed desperate and nervous. He wouldn't explain to me what exactly he needed the money for. Just kept saying that it was an emergency and he needed it immediately."

"Is it abnormal for your son to go months without speaking to you?"

"He is… *was*… an emotional boy. His feelings are hurt easily, and he doesn't know how to address them." This was the first hint of grief the pair had heard from Mrs. DeCordts, but it didn't last long. "He was soft."

"Who would want him dead, Cheryl? The way he died was vicious. Whoever did this must have been angry with him."

"I couldn't tell you, Tingles," she said "Many people hated my entire family after my husband's run-in with the law. None of us ever *really* recovered from it." As she finished her sentence Tingles noticed that she, again, was glaring at him.

"Do you think, Cheryl, your son's murder could be connected to your husband?"

"I can't think of any reason it would. Can you?" Perhaps the interrogation was turning on Tingles.

"The address the young woman who bought a safe deposit box gave is yours. The head in the safe deposit box was your son's. Those aren't coincidences, Mrs. DeCordts. Someone is targeting your family, and we need you to help us figure out *why*."

"I have no idea. Outside of a wrongful accusation of murder against my husband over thirty years ago, I can't come up with a single thing someone would hate us enough for to murder one of us." Her words were pointed, and Tingles temporarily believed her.

"Mrs. DeCordts," Gentry said. Tingles had nearly forgotten he was in the room. "Please think carefully about this. Mr. Tingles is right that someone is targeting your family which means you could be in danger. Best case scenario is this is a warning. Worst case scenario, it's a plot for vengeance. Now, can you think of *anyone* who would want to hurt your family?"

"I don't know, Detective," Cheryl said confidently. "I can't think of anything that helps make sense of this."

The detectives thanked Mrs. DeCordts for her time and

rose to see themselves out. When they got to the doorway Mr. Tingles turned around and said, "One last question. Where can we find your son, Joseph?"

Without turning to face him Mrs. DeCordts replied, "I'm not sure, Detective. He doesn't speak to me either."

Detective Gentry and Mr. Tingles made the long journey from the front porch of the DeCordts' home to the black SUV and hoisted themselves into it. Mr. Tingles, having left Gentry out of his plan to interrogate Mrs. DeCordts was already knee-deep in contemplation about what she could have been hiding from them. Tingles could tell Gentry, on the other hand, was confused and frustrated. It was understandable, Tingles thought. From the moment he'd arrived, Gentry probably felt like he had been working the case without any consideration of him or his force. He had a tendency to take over investigations. While they'd called him in because they were in over their heads, it was still *their* case. His handling of the questioning of Mrs. DeCordts was the behavior of a rogue detective, but Tingles knew it was necessary to get Mrs. DeCordts talking. People like her could smell weakness and timidity; to assert one's dominance over them, a detective had to be direct, even brutal in their questioning. The energy in the SUV was palpable. Mr. Tingles deep in thought, Detective Gentry deep in resentment.

"Tingles, what the fuck was that?" Gentry snipped, breaking the silence they'd sat in for several minutes.

"What was… what?" Tingles asked innocently, but grinning coyly.

"We just went in there to tell her that her son was murdered, and you attacked her. What the fuck was *that?*"

"Gentry," Tingles started, looking him in the eye. "I apologize for not being clearer on my intentions. I planned to interrogate Mrs. DeCordts before we ever arrived. It was the perfect time. I anticipated she wouldn't give us a reaction to this news – not because I think she's guilty, but because I still believe she's hiding something. When we told her Darren Southern, her late husband's business partner and a family friend, had been murdered she reacted the same. She continued to behave in that manner throughout the entire investigation. I knew that if she reacted similarly to this news I could guarantee my instincts about this case being related to her husbands are right. She was hiding something then and she's hiding something now. The next thing we have to do is continue questioning everyone involved in the DeCordts case. I promise you, Detective – the key to the new case lies in the old one."

"You can't just go rogue on me, Tingles," Gentry responded. "You have to share your plans with me. Surprise me again and I'm sending your ass home. You understand me?"

"10-4," Tingles responded, noting Gentry didn't argue with any of his points.

Detective Gentry put the SUV in drive and headed back towards the station. Tingles was right, of course, that they needed to get moving on their questioning of other potential witnesses. If they were going to connect a murder from over three decades ago to their current case, they had a lot of work ahead. Tingles knew Gentry didn't think his ultimatum for him had been taken seriously. They both knew Tingles was no fool — they needed him, and Tingles knew that. They were both also wholly aware that he wouldn't, indeed, send Tingle's ass home if he went rogue again.

Within minutes the duo arrived at Brent DeCordts' house. Like the home he'd grown up in, and like many others in the neighborhood where he and his mother lived, Brent's was a 1940's-style structure. There was a small neighborhood in Reidsville that the wealthy occupied - lawyers, doctors, politicians, bankers, and a couple of heiresses — but all of their homes looked alike. Gentry couldn't help thinking it was odd Mrs. DeCordts hadn't seen or spoken to the son who lived less than five minutes from her. How had he managed to avoid her? He filed the thought away for future consideration and approached the front entrance of Brent

DeCordts' home. Police caution tape was wrapped around the perimeter of the property, and it was swarming with officers (to the degree a small town with limited police resources can be *swarmed* with officers). Tingles had stopped in the middle of the yard and was looking back and forth from Brent's yard to the direction of Mrs. DeCordts' home. He was wearing his "I'm on to something" face, one that even Isaiah had come to recognize.

"What ya' got?" Gentry asked Tingles from the front porch. Tingles either ignored or hadn't heard him. He kept moving his head back and forth and had begun mouthing something to himself. Gentry left him alone until he was ready to talk and proceeded into Brent's home.

Inside the house, he found Officers Johnson and Carter. Johnson stood in the entryway giving orders. Carter appeared to be organizing evidence bags. A few scattered officers looked to be lifting prints, tagging areas of the home, and sifting through documents. Gentry noticed immediately that nothing looked out of place other than the officers and what they'd disturbed. Without speaking to Johnson or Carter, he headed up the stairway from the bottom floor up to an impressive landing. There were no officers on the upper level yet, and he wanted to test a theory - was this house even lived in? He slowly walked through the hall, looking in every room on his way. He noticed a thick layer of dust on nearly everything. It appeared the rooms had not only been unlived in but gone un-cleaned for months. Gentry found what he thought would have been Brent's bedroom. He slowly walked through it, careful not to disturb anything that might be evidence. He saw a phone charger on the nightstand, a handful of ties draped over the corner of the mirror standing next to the closet door, and a pair of pants draped over the bench at the end of the bed – all covered with a layer of dust. On top of the dresser, there was a collection of watches that had been placed haphazardly on a display stand. Other than these observations, there was nothing to be said of the bedroom or other rooms on the floor. Gentry felt vindicated in his initial reaction - no one had lived in this home for a long time.

As soon as he hit the landing at the top of the staircase, he saw Tingles come through the door. Tingles noticed Gentry immediately, and the two of them said simultaneously, "I think I've got something." Gentry gestured for Tingles to come up to the second floor. As the two arrived in the second-story hallway Gentry began explaining that he believed the home to be un-lived in, pointing out the thin layers of dust on everything. He walked Tingles through the items in the bedroom and concluded by showing him the closet - empty. Tingles was silent while Gentry spoke, except muttering "mhm" and "I agree." At a minimum, this home had been vacant for months. When Gentry probed Tingles for the "something" he was onto, he was silent. He'd walked back into the hallway, looking again from side to side and again started mouthing something to himself.

"Tingles, talk to me," Gentry said, breaking a deafening silence.

"Oh," he replied, seemingly snapping back from an alternate universe. "Yes. You're right, Detective, that this home looks like it was abandoned long before Mr. DeCordts' murder occurred, begging the question, "Where was he living?" Those pants, one of those watches, and one of the ties were likely the last things he wore on the last day he was here. Did he leave intentionally or was he kidnapped? We also need to figure out how long he's been gone. Have someone pull his bank records for the past twelve months - his spending history will tell a story. We need someone to lift prints in this room. If he was kidnapped it was from this room, and we may luck up with finding someone else's prints. I'm especially interested in whether there are any prints in that closet. Very strange that it's been emptied…" Tingles' voice trailed off, and he was lost in thought again. Still standing in the hallway he was looking back and forth again.

"What are you thinking, Tingles?" Gentry asked. "You've been turning your head back and forth like a bobblehead since we got here."

"Did you know that you can see Mrs. DeCordts'

home from the front yard *and* from this hallway? As a matter of fact, the window at the end of this hallway looks directly to the second-story window of her second-story hallway window."

"Okay…" Gentry said. It was more of a question as he was uncertain what Tingles was saying.

"Mrs. DeCordts told us," Tingles started, erring on the side of condescending, "that she hadn't seen her son in months. There would normally be two problems with that story. First, the clear line of vision between these two homes. There's no way, as close as they are and with the view of one from the other, she wouldn't have at least seen her son coming or going. Secondly, there are handprints in the dust on the windowsill of the hallway window. Someone has been standing at that window looking towards mama's house. They appear to be too small for a man. So, now we need to know who they belong to. It appears we have more questions than answers."

As Tingles finished his thought, he became distracted by something in the bedroom. Gentry followed his eyes to the corner of the floor in the closet and immediately saw what he hadn't noticed initially. A small red flower petal. "Is that…?" Gentry started. Tingles shook his head and finished the sentence.

"Evita."

CHAPTER SIX

ack at the station, Tingles and Gentry settled in a conference room. The walls were lined with whiteboards where they had begun mapping out their theories, activities, and to-do's. On the board in the middle, Tingles had written the following:

1989 Murder of Darren M. Southern
Primary Suspect: Paul DeCordts

←————------ 2023 Murder of Brent DeCordts
Primary Suspect: Unknown ————------>

Officers Johnson and Carter entered the room behind Detective Gentry and took seats facing the boards. Tingles was standing, ready to debrief the officers on what they knew and what they needed to know. He'd removed his suit jacket, revealing a light gray and blue pin-striped vest with a baby-blue button-down shirt and matching bowtie. He still donned his fedora with peacock feathers erupting from its side. Once everyone was settled Tingles began:

"Good afternoon, gentlemen. I won't waste time beating around the bush. Here's what we've got. Brent DeCordts' head was found on August 5th, 2023. Approximately three months prior he asked his mother for money, was denied, and wasn't seen or heard from by his mother after. Officer Johnson questioned Brent's friend and business partner, and we have no reason to believe he's involved. He hadn't seen or heard from Brent in the past several months either as he had stepped away from the everyday operations of the business. Mr. DeCordts' home appears to have not been lived in for several months, as is evident by the layers of dust on most of the surfaces. Inside the home we found a petal from a *seemannia nematanthodes* flower, otherwise known as Evita - the same type of flower found in the hair of Mr. DeCordts' decapitated head. Finally, we found handprints in the dust on the windowsill of Mr. DeCordts' second-story hallway window - the same window that looks directly up the street into the second-story window of his mother's home. The handprints are too small to be Mr. DeCordts', and very fresh, meaning someone has been in the home looking out that window in the past few weeks. Whoever that person is may likely be our suspect given the same flower petal was found at both scenes."

Tingles paused - for questions or dramatic effect, the room wasn't sure - though, given the peacock feathers blowing in the breeze of the overhead fan, it was hard not to believe it wasn't for dramatic effect. He started again so quickly it startled everyone.

"As I have said these past few days, I believe this murder is connected to that of Mr. Darren M. Southern. He was murdered in 1989, and my primary suspect was Paul DeCordts. To solve *this* case, we need to re-investigate the murder of Darren M. Southern." Johnson had raised his hand like an eighth-grade student and Tingles paused for his question.

"Were no prints found? I mean, we've got handprints but no fingerprints?" he asked.

"Whoever left them must have been wearing gloves," Tingles replied.

Johnson raised his hand again and Mr. Tingles narrowed his eyes at him.

"This is a police station, Officer Johnson, not an elementary school classroom. Hand raising won't be necessary."

"And is this Mr. Southern related to the people who own the Southern Bank?" Johnson asked, narrowing his eyes back at Mr. Tingles and smirking.

"Good catch, Sherlock. Indeed, he was. Darren Southern was the great-grandchild of the founder of

Southern Bank."

"I don't think it's a coincidence that the head was found *there* considering the relation to the initial case," Johnson stated. "Do you?"

"I'm not sure yet," Tingles responded. "To make that connection we need to question Darren Southern's widow." With this, Tingles took a seat across from the others, the white boards tall behind him. "We need to see what Mrs. Southern remembers about her husband's murder. Let's also track down Brent's twin, Joseph."

"We're going to have a major issue with questioning the widow," Carter spoke up.

"Why is that?" Gentry asked.

"She ain't lived here since the murder. No one's heard from her or seen her in years. Went completely off the grid. It's stuff of local legend."

"That does pose a problem, indeed," Tingles said. "Let's pull the case notes from the department, compare them to mine, and see if we can put together a narrative that gives us something we didn't already have.

"Back then, Mrs. Southern didn't have much to offer. She'd been out of the house that evening at a gala, an alibi that checked out twenty times over. So, she was never a suspect. Let's also look at the statements her alibis provided and see if there are any gaps."

Tingles knew there were no gaps in the witness

statements for Mrs. Southern. He'd been over them hundreds of times, including those recent reviews the evening before. He wasn't stupid, though. Two sets of eyes were better than one even when you were as sure of yourself as he was. Detective Gentry, seemingly done with the back and forth, stood and began distributing orders.

"Johnson, pull the case files for the department and have someone start reviewing them. Then see if we can find Mrs. Southern. Officer Carter, you're on the witness statements for her alibi for the night of her husband's murder - look for any inconsistencies or gaps in the information provided. Tingles, you and I will find Joseph DeCordts and have a chat with him."

"Before we all go our separate ways," Tingles interjected, "may I offer one more *teensy* bit of insight?"

"Shoot," Gentry said pointedly.

"We have nothing so far except questions about questions. If we don't move swiftly and efficiently, we'll continue to collect questions without answers. I would recommend having one of these fine officers follow up on the camera footage from the bank so we can try to identify the woman who dropped off the head. We should also find the closest florist who sells *seemannia nematanthodes*. We've found the flower at two scenes related to this case, so it must mean something. If we can't find our suspect through forensics, we'll have to follow the clues. There's always a story, gentleman. It's our job to find it and tell it. Lastly, someone should put together a statement for Kimmie Flague before she barges in here again and causes a scene. The more control we take over what she knows and when, the easier our job will be."

Tingles' statement caused Detective Gentry to rethink his orders and reallocate-responsibilities. Tingles was right again. They had more questions than answers, and their leads thus far were ambiguous at best. Tingles could tell Gentry, so overwhelmed by a case much too big for his small police force, had nearly forgotten about identifying the woman who'd delivered the head to Southern Bank. It was moments like these where Tingles had experienced imposter syndrome early in his career and wished he'd had someone like himself to gently and respectfully put him on track. Thoughts like: "What am I doing here that I can't even remember to identify the only viable suspect we have in the murder and dismemberment of another human being?" had clouded his judgment and led to some rookie mistakes. He wouldn't allow that to happen to Isaiah. Not only did he have the opportunity to solve one of the few cases had gone unsolved in his career, but he also had a chance to mentor a young detective – a young *gay* detective. If anyone knew how important that task was it was Leroy H. Tingles, IV.

As Officers Johnson and Carter headed to complete their tasks Tingles noticed Isaiah had become somber, placing his hands over his head and breathing deeply.

"Detective, are you alright?" Tingles asked.

"Oh, sure," Isaiah said sarcastically. "Tingles, what the fuck am I doing here?" He rose and moved swiftly past him out of the room, brushing Donna who was approaching the doorway.

"He alright?" she asked Tingles.

"He will be," Tingles replied softly. "He's feeling a little... in over his head."

"Poor thing," Donna said. "He's a good kid. Been through a lot and really trying to find his way. Glad he's got you."

"Sounds like he's lucky to have you, too," Tingles said. "I'll go check on him in a few minutes. I think he needs some time alone."

"I'll go make him some coffee. That always cheers him up," Donna replied, leaving.

The embarrassment Isaiah likely felt was one Tingles knew well. The feeling of inadequacy and shame was one he also knew all too well – most gay men do. Isaiah reminded Tingles of himself; he likely felt like he had something to prove – to his parents, to his town, and most importantly to himself. Tingles could relate to the feeling of not belonging anywhere you go and the feeling that no matter what you do (or how well you do it) it's not good enough, and the feeling that any mistake one makes will eclipse any success one has had. Though Tingles had given Isaiah the time and autonomy to ensure he followed up on identifying the suspect, he acknowledged to himself he'd been condescending towards him and his force and owed them an apology. Tingles had taken for granted he'd worked many cases such as this and Isaiah and his force hadn't. With this in mind, Tingles left the room and searched for Isaiah, finding him in the restroom, two cups of coffee in hand.

Gentry stood in front of the bathroom mirror looking at his chiseled features. Moments before he'd splashed cold water on his smooth skin and patted it dry, leaving a slight gleam to it. He was twenty-eight years old and not only the youngest detective the Reidsville Police Department had ever had, but almost certainly the only gay one. *"You've got to get your shit together,"* he said aloud to himself.

"Donna made you coffee," Tingles said. "If you want it." Mr. Tingles' southern drawl echoed through the walls of the bathroom and startled Detective Gentry who didn't realize he'd been speaking aloud. He didn't turn around but looked up at the mirror to see Tingles' reflection. He didn't respond, leaving Tingles with two hot cups of coffee in his hands.

"You are here because you belong here. You can do this."

Isaiah scoffed at Tingles' words of encouragement. "Respectfully," he started, "I forgot about identifying the suspect. That's *less* than a rookie mistake. It's like a fucking six-year-old running this investigation."

"Oh, poppycock!" Tingles exclaimed, chuckling. "Indeed, you can do this. You're a good detective, Isaiah. I hope it's alright for me to call you by your first name - we are going to be spending a lot of time together, after all."

Mr. Tingles didn't give Isaiah much time to respond before he continued:

"I remember when I was a new detective. It wasn't far from here in Greensboro. I had been a beat cop for several years - made the most arrests of any beat cop in their history, and I still hold that title. Not bullshit arrests, either, for weed or loitering – you know the type of arrests that are just intended to meet quotas and oppress minorities. But I digress... It was never enough, though. Every arrest I made was motivated by the need to prove myself wrong. Every day I clocked in with the goal of proving myself to everyone - including myself. Then I became a detective, and my success continued. I solved every case except for three. I've written best-selling books, spoken at universities across the country, won a shit-ton of awards, and am highly respected in our field. Bet you can't guess what I think about when I'm all alone thinking about my illustrious career."

Tingles let his last sentence hang in the air between his mouth and Isaiah's back. Isaiah continued to look at Tingles' reflection. After several moments Tingles spoke again.

"Those three unsolved cases," he said quietly, his voice no longer echoing against the cream-colored tile walls. One of the toilets began flushing softly, breaking the awkward silence. Outside the door they heard the muffled voices; together with the running toilet and their soft breathing, a symphony of white noise emerged and played for several minutes.

"What I'm trying to say is this," Tingles started again, now walking closer to Isaiah. "Give yourself a little grace. I know how it feels to be young, queer, not accepted by your family, and trying to prove yourself. If there's anything you can learn from me, it's that you don't have to prove anything to anyone but yourself. And one thing I've learned about you in the past few days is you're smart, capable, determined, and you belong here. I see myself in you, really. And I turned out pretty damn good."

Isaiah had turned to face Mr. Tingles. He was appreciative of his peptalk.

"As you know, I was outed by Kimmie Flague when I was seventeen. For a little over a decade, I've been trying to figure out how to live as a gay man in the Bible Belt. I haven't been exposed to... well, *anything* to do with being gay except when the pastor at my childhood church reminded the congregation that the *"fags would burn in hell for their perversion."* I don't know any other queer people, haven't really seen any shows with queer people, read any books with queer content, and haven't stepped foot in many queer spaces. In fact, the most exposure I've had to queer culture to this very moment was one night spent in a queer nightclub and a few hookups. Hell, I still don't know if I'm a top or bottom. I've spent my entire life feeling embarrassed and ashamed of my identity. I've spent more time trying to cover it up than I have exploring it. Living life as an openly gay male while simultaneously having no understanding of it is the most bizarre feeling of my life."

Mr. Tingles wanted to hug Isaiah, an impulse that wasn't natural for him. He wasn't an affectionate person, but for the first time in his life, he felt connected to a person in the way he thought a father might feel a connection to his son. He resisted the urge to hug Isaiah, instead waiting for him to finish his thoughts.

"Thank you, Mr. Tingles. It's refreshing to have someone who understands some of what I've gone through and how that might make one feel…."

"Out of place?" Tingles offered.

"Yeah, something like that," Isaiah said. "I just want to get this right, you know?"

"I do know. You will, young man. Together, we're going to catch the sons-of-bitches who murdered these people."

At that moment they heard Johnson's voice in the hallway asking if anyone had seen Gentry and Tingles.

Immediately, Mr. Tingles thought how awkward it would be for them to walk out of the bathroom together. He could hear it now: *The two homos were in the bathroom together.* He noticed Isaiah's expression.

"You go first. I'll give you a couple of minutes to get him in your office and then join you," Tingles said, handing Gentry a cup of coffee.

Gentry reached the door and placed his hand on the knob, pausing. He took a deep breath to recover from the emotions he'd been feeling.

"Although," Tingles began, "it would be quite the scandal if we just walked out together."

Gentry looked back at Tingles, and they shared a smile.

"You know," Mr. Tingles said, "I think you're starting to like me."

CHAPTER SEVEN

By the time Tingles made it to Gentry's office, Officer Johnson was mid-way through his update.

"We found *one* source locally for see…. Seeman…

"Oooh, I came in at just the right time…" Tingles said cheekily, startling Officer Johnson who, upon processing his statement blushed and continued:

"That damn Madonna flower. It's a greenhouse on the outskirts of town which specializes in rare flowers. I've got Carter getting the owner's name and a little information before we barge in there. Also, no viable fingerprints at the scene."

"Anything on the camera footage at the bank?" Gentry asked.

"In your inbox now. They sent over some stills, too, though the woman's face isn't clear enough to get an I.D."

"Y'all work fast," Mr. Tingles said, surprised. Only an hour had passed since they met in the conference room, and they'd already checked off some important items on their to-do list.

"We may be hillbillies, Tingles, but we're competent," Johnson responded as he turned and left. The comment was tongue-in-cheek. Even Johnson had let go of much of his animosity towards Tingles. He'd been the one to suggest bringing him in. Not only had he learned he was a good detective, but he refused to be wrong by showing any ill will towards the man.

The two detectives took their place behind the office desk after Isaiah suggested they look at the footage and stills he'd received. Even if they couldn't get a sketch out of it, there may be something they could use. While they waited for Isaiah's computer to load, he filled in Mr. Tingles on the first half of Johnson's update. They'd obtained Brent DeCordts' bank statements and were putting together a narrative, but according to what they'd reviewed so far there was nothing to tell. Brent's credit cards were used up until his approximate time of death. Joseph DeCordts hadn't been located. It turned out he hadn't been seen or heard from since his father's death the previous year. All his bank accounts had been closed, he'd sold his home, and the new address on every document he'd signed was now occupied by someone named Irene Mallard. The two agreed Joseph wiping himself off the grid was strange and noted how they'd need to push the force until they found him. Taking so much care to disappear wasn't the behavior of an innocent man, but they also knew if he was involved he wasn't doing it alone. They still had a female on camera delivering a decapitated head. By the time Mr. Tingles was filled in and they'd discussed their thoughts on the updates, Isaiah's computer had loaded. He navigated to his email, found the one he was looking for and loaded the footage. The top right corner of the screen read "Gigi's Floral Fabulosity, 8-1-23, 02:05:44." Tingles remembered the bank had very few cameras, none of which were outside. Gigi's Floral Fabulosity was across the street from the bank. If they had to obtain footage from a business around, that was the best place to get it from.

The footage showed a woman in a flowing blue sundress. The footage was slightly grainy but from what the two saw her skin appeared to be smooth and porcelain. Gentry and Tingles agreed she was definitely young. Her hair was long and blonde, cascading down her back from underneath a large straw sunhat. The hat shielded her face from the sun, and the camera; a large pair of black sunglasses finished the job of anonymizing her. The woman carried a large purse over her shoulder, presumably containing Brent DeCordts' head. The clip, less than a minute long, was less helpful than Isaiah hoped. All they knew was the bank manager, Sheila Flague, had been truthful when she said the woman was white and blonde. After viewing the footage Isaiah opened the file with the stills of the woman. They were from a different angle, and the two could see the woman from the front. Mr. Tingles leaned into the computer screen, slowly gasping.

"Do you see what I see?" he asked Gentry.

"Madonna," Gentry replied, referring to the bright red flower on the straw hat on their suspect's head, and smirking at Tingles.

"Bingo. We need to visit that greenhouse ASAP. I'm willing to bet our suspect found Evita from them." He paused. "*Madonna.* Psht. I'd even settle for Elaine Paige."

"Should we circulate this image in the media and see if anyone can help us find her?" Gentry asked, ignoring Tingles' disdain of Madonna.

"Not just yet," Tingles responded. "We don't want her to get antsy. She's leaving clues for us which tells me it's a game to her. She wants us to figure it out, but she doesn't want to get caught, and she's been very careful about that. If we let her know we're on to her, she may get nervous and become more reckless. I also have the sense she's trying to help us."

"Help us?" Gentry was confused.

"I do not think the person who murdered Darren Southern murdered Brent DeCordts. I do think whoever murdered Brent knows who murdered Darren."

"So, you think Brent's murder is a revenge kill?"

"I'm not sure yet. But I'd bet my bottom dollar I'm right about our latest killer knowing our older one."

"So, now we're working backward instead of working from 1989 forward?" Gentry was one part toying with Tingles and one part genuinely curious.

"Both. We should continue looking through the notes from the original case while continuing to follow the leads we have currently. They'll meet in the middle, I'm sure of it."

Isaiah felt energized. They'd discovered the first important lead. Their primary suspect was seen wearing a hat with the same type of rare flower which had been found with the decapitated head, and in the home of the deceased. Then they'd identified a single local source who grew rare flowers. For the first time since August 5th, Isaiah felt like he was part of something that was making a difference. They were going to catch a killer.

He and Tingles decided to visit the greenhouse on the edge of town the following morning. They'd spend what was left of the afternoon reviewing case notes from the Southern murder to identify any gaps or missed opportunities. They ordered Chinese take-out from a mediocre joint in town and settled down in the conference room. As the sun began to set, they both started yawning.

Gentry was seconds from calling it quits when he noticed the paper in his hand was thicker than a single sheet should be. He peered at its edge, confirming there was a page stuck to it. Carefully peeling the pages apart, he notified Tingles of his finding who watched with bated breath - he was more concerned Gentry's man-hands would tear the sheets in half than he was that there would be anything valuable on it.

Gentry finally peeled the two pages apart and laid them side by side. He spent a couple of minutes looking over them, deciding they weren't important. Tingles, however, reached across the conference room table and asked to take a look. After several moments - not minutes - Tingles looked up over his glasses and smirked.

"There is something here I missed in 1989, young man."

"What is it?" Gentry asked excitedly.

"The Southerns had a daughter. She was three years old at the time of her father's murder. This sheet says she was never questioned due to her age. Sounds like we have another person to find."

CHAPTER EIGHT

The workday had come and gone, and Gentry and Tingles found themselves mentally exhausted. The two had spent their day knee-deep in what little evidence they'd been able to find, the clues they'd identified, and their theories about what could be motivating their current killer. Tingles couldn't help thinking he'd never seen a case like this before. They had a handful of confusing clues – both new and old – and nothing else. At the same time, they had enough to know that two murders, separated by thirty-five years, were connected. Tingles found himself frustrated. How could two murderers be so good at evading suspicion? After nearly an hour of silence, save for the turning of papers from the original case files, Tingles spoke.

"I could really use a big, stiff co…"

"Whoa!" Gentry said, his cheeks blood-red with embarrassment over what he thought Tingles was about to say.

"...cktail," Tingles finished, dropping his head in confusion. But then immediately he looked offended.

"Sorry," Gentry said, embarrassed now for a different reason. "I thought you were going to say something…"

"Vulgar?" Tingles asked. "Have I given you any reason to think *I'd* be saying something like that?"

"I… no. I guess not," Gentry replied. "I don't know, it's just that you're so…"

"Gay?" Tingles said sarcastically.

"No… I mean, yes," Gentry said, fumbling through his thoughts. "But it's not just that."

The tension in the room had suddenly become palpable. Their days of exhaustion and tireless work culminated in a moment of friction between two generations of queer men. Tingles knew what was happening, but Gentry wasn't aware yet. Tingles had encountered these conflicts with young queer people before - mostly young, queer, white men. He knew the type. Young queer men from small southern towns who were one less episode of *Dynasty* away from convincing themselves they were actually heterosexual. Therefore, they clung to every stereotypical idea of masculinity they'd heard from church pulpits and tobacco fields as a security blanket. No matter how many other queer men they met, if they weren't "as gay" as them, they felt better about themselves. Meanwhile, the queer men like Tingles who wore their sexual and gender identities on their sleeves had judgment and discrimination against them from inside *and* outside the house. The only difference between a twenty-three-year-old flamboyant queer man and the sixty-three-year-old flamboyant queer man was that sixty-three-year-old Tingles was always prepared for these conversations.

"Isaiah, let me save you the trouble of trying to pinpoint what it is about me you don't like," Tingles said.

"Look, Ting…"

"I'm nowhere near done, young man."

Tingles rose and rounded the conference room table which had separated the two men. He sat down next to Gentry and turned his chair to face him thinking he hadn't planned on two heart-to-hearts with him in one day. He'd learned many lessons about how to have these conversations with young queer men. Anger had never done the trick, so he'd found a way to deliver his message in a fatherly manner. The young people on the receiving end of these conversations usually needed a parental figure, he'd discovered, and in addition to solving murders, he thought it was his calling to provide that to those who needed it.

"Look, Isaiah," he started. "I know people like me are hard for some to understand. I'm flamboyant, sassy, confident, feminine, loud, and just generally take up a lot of physical and audible space. What you don't know is it has taken me a lifetime to figure out it's okay for me to be all of those things. You're still young, and still trying to figure out who you are in this world. That's normal. But you need to know there is enough space in this wide world for who you are *and* who I am. Nothing about me makes it harder for you to be who you are. So, I would just appreciate it if you'd be more respectful going forward, otherwise, I will have to leave. I've worked too hard to love myself to be disrespected by a member of my own community."

There'd been several minutes of silence following Tingles' monologue. Gentry looked positively embarrassed and was struggling with the idea he'd been a bully to a sixty-three-year-old man who'd put him in his place.

"I'm sorry, Tingles," he finally said. "Like I said earlier, I don't know how to be gay. I don't know anything about this world. All I know is I find other men incredibly attractive and when I envision a life with a partner, that partner is a man. I don't know shit about Bette Davis, or Evita, or gay slang, books, movies, music, or any of it."

"Well," Tingles said. "First of all, there's no right way to be gay. You don't need to know who Bette Davis is to be gay." He laughed. "But secondly, and more importantly, it's never too late to learn whatever you want to learn."

"I have an idea if you're game," Gentry said, and Tingles nodded avidly. "Why don't we find one of these

Bette Davis movies to stream, grab some bottles, and have some cock..." he paused, and Tingles laughed again, "...tails."

"I'd like that very much," Tingles said. "Let's get the hell out of here."

The two of them stopped by Gentry's house and grabbed a couple of bottles of liquor - bourbon for Tingles and rum for Gentry. When they arrived at the Reidsville Inn and settled in with their drinks and gas station snacks, Tingles opened Gentry's laptop and found Amazon Prime video.

"Alright, young man," Tingles said. "I am going to give you a Queer 101 lesson and show you *All About Eve*. It is the quintessential Bette Davis film. Made when she was in her prime, it was her comeback film. She should have won the Oscar, but she was beat out by that damned Judy Holiday. *Judy Holiday* - I'd have understood if she was up against Judy *Garland*."

Tingles saw how Gentry was looking at him with a confused expression. He'd lost the room, so to speak, but was expecting that to happen.

"Oh, don't worry, Isaiah," Tingles said. "I'll teach you everything you want to know, but today's lesson is a forced one because you can't be queer and have never seen *All About Eve* — that's the *only rule!* So, without further ado, *fasten your seatbelts... it's going to be a bumpy night.*"

"That wasn't so bad," Gentry commented as the credits rolled. "Bette Davis is a little bit of a badass, huh?"

"Oh, you have no idea," Tingles said. "She was bona fide badass in real life, too. A woman who paved the way for other women in the entertainment industry."

"I like that," Gentry replied. "A strong woman who cared enough to make it possible for other women to be successful."

"Well, I don't know that she cared enough, necessarily. Sometimes we can make a huge difference just by being true to ourselves, and I think that's what she was doing. She refused to settle for 'no,' or to not get the same opportunities as men. She *was* strong, but I don't think it was for anyone but her. Not directly."

"I don't know, Tingles," Gentry said. "I see a little of her in you, you know?"

Tingles looked over at him, surprised.

"What do you mean?" he asked.

"I mean, you're strong, too. You live your life authentically and true to yourself. And that's made it possible for little shits like me to walk in your shadow."

"Oh," Tingles said, seemingly embarrassed by Gentry's words. "I think there's a little difference."

"How so?"

The room fell silent for a few moments and Gentry felt the mood in the room become more somber. He was in for the third life lesson of the day.

"Well, you're right. I live authentically and am unapologetic about who I am," Tingles said. "But a lot of what I do is intentional. It's for those little queer kids in small southern towns like you and me. It's to show them we are more than what the world makes us out to be. We are more than our oppression, more than our hurt, and more than our fear. It ain't easy to be this gay."

"I know I don't know much about our community - but thank you. Thank you for what you've done for people like me."

"It's what I live for," Tingles said. "Now get the hell out of here. We've got another long day tomorrow."

CHAPTER NINE

The evening came and went. Neither Tingles nor Gentry slept well in anticipation of the day ahead. To be sure, the bourbon and rum didn't help. Gentry offered to come back and pick Tingles up at the Reidsville Inn at 6:30am. They'd stop for coffee to-go and head to the greenhouse first thing. The greenhouse was owned by an elderly woman named Martha Raines, who'd been growing rare North Carolinian flowers for over thirty years. Gentry pointed out the evening before how they needed to know if Martha was a private seller or a wholesaler. If she distributed to florists all over the county, or farther, they had a bigger pool of possibilities. If she only sold to folks in the county, it would be easier to narrow her clientele down. Each agreed Martha, herself, was likely not their suspect, but Tingles had been surprised before, so he reminded Gentry to keep an open mind.

At 6:30am on the dot Gentry parked in front of Mr. Tingles' motel room, who emerged from the doorway in a light pink suit with cream accessories and a cream minicape. His matching fedora featured several pheasant feathers. Tingles climbed in the SUV, moving the pheasant feathers out of the way of the vehicle as he did, and they headed toward the Java J. Coffee Spot. They rode mostly in silence to the coffee shop and then to the greenhouse, save for a few morning pleasantries. They were both sleepy and saving their energy for Martha. Their destination was much farther than they were accustomed to traveling over the past few days. Reidsville had a small population, but a lot of land. Traveling to "the edge of town" felt like they were traveling to the edge of the universe. When they finally arrived at the greenhouse, the sun had risen, and the August heat was already setting in.

Tingles, as usual, was the first at the door of the greenhouse. He was small but fast. He peered through the windows and, seeing no one inside, looked around the property. Through a patch of trees, the two spotted a small cottage where Martha must have lived. They made eye contact and agreed silently to make their way to the cottage, but Tingles didn't make haste this time. He slowly walked by the greenhouse taking inventory of the plants he recognized. He was almost at the end when he saw it: Evita. Once he was satisfied that they were, indeed, at the right greenhouse, he caught up to Gentry and they walked together to the cottage.

Tingles knocked softly on the door - it was only 7am after all. They heard footsteps on what was presumably a wood floor, but no one came to the door. The pair looked at each other quizzically and shrugged. Gentry knocked on the door this time, and louder, but this time there were no footsteps. Suddenly they heard snapping twigs behind them and turned to face the barrel of a shotgun.

"Whoa!" Gentry said, his voice cracking slightly as the exclamation was only about the tenth word he'd spoken all day. He drew his own weapon and pointed it at the woman.

It's too early, and I'm too hungover for this shit, he thought.

"My name is Detective Isaiah Gentry, and this is Detective Tingles. We are actively investigating the homicide of a local resident and think you can help. I'm going to ask you to lower the weapon, Ms. Raines."

"Who told you to come here?" Martha barked. She was in her sixties, stood approximately five feet tall, and was as round as she was tall. Her long gray hair framed her plump and wrinkled face in a most unflattering way. Tingles thought she looked like a character from *The Hills Have Eyes* and wondered who would buy flowers from a woman so unpleasant.

"I don't know shit about no murder," she said, not allowing the detectives to answer her question, and not bothering to heed Gentry's warning to lower her weapon.

"Ms. Raines, lower your weapon now," Gentry ordered, noticing that as he spoke, Tingles was taking small steps forward.

"*What the fuck are you doing?*" he whispered out of the corner of his mouth. Tingles didn't respond but spoke to Martha.

"Martha, like my colleague said, my name is Detective Tingles, but you can just call me Mr. Tingles. I'm sorry we surprised you this morning - we know it's very early, but we wanted to be sure we caught you while you're at home, and before you get too busy. If it's alright with you, we'd like to ask a few questions of you. You may know something that you don't realize is helpful to us. Would that be okay?"

Mr. Tingles' words settled in the air between the three of them for what felt like hours. Martha looked back and forth at Tingles and Gentry, who still had his weapon drawn. Tingles thought it felt like a showdown in the Wild West. Gentry thought he'd rather still be in bed. Finally, Martha began lowering the shotgun. Mr. Tingles asked, "Is it alright if I hold your weapon while we talk?"

Oh sure, Gentry thought. *She'll just hand you....*

To his utter shock, Martha placed the shotgun on the ground and kicked it towards Tingles' feet. He thanked her, picked up the weapon, and handed it to Gentry, who was ready to slap handcuffs on her. Tingles beat him to her, though.

"Martha, under normal circumstances we'd have to arrest you for pulling a weapon on a police detective," he said.

She looked furious at this statement.

"However," Tingles continued, noting her face soften at the hint of an exception, "we need your help. So, if you cooperate, we will not arrest you. If you don't, we will. If we find out you lied to us or withheld information, we'll come back and arrest you. Do you understand?"

Gentry looked at Tingles, a little shocked. Isaiah hadn't seen this side of him before. The Tingles he knew to be flamboyant, sassy, and exhibit southern charm like he was competing for a grand prize in it had become stern, assertive, and frankly, a little scary – despite his baby pink suit and pheasant feathers blowing in the morning breeze. Tingles could tell Gentry was impressed by how he was handling what could have been an otherwise violent and unfortunate circumstance. Tingles could also tell Gentry wasn't upset that he'd gone rogue again - there hadn't been time to devise a plan, and apparently, neither of them counted on Ms. Raines pulling a shotgun on them.

Martha nodded in agreement with Mr. Tingles' terms and grunted for them to follow her. She pivoted on her heels and walked back towards the greenhouse they'd come from. As the detectives trailed behind her, they exchanged looks that said, "What the fuck just happened?" They observed Martha, noting her long gray hair, her oversized nightgown, the front of which was stained with food, and her fluffy cat bedroom shoes. It was apparent she either hadn't been awake very long or, because she worked at home alone, simply didn't take good care of herself. They also couldn't help but notice the stench coming from her and Tingles decided her appearance was likely best explained by the latter. Martha arrived at the greenhouse door and dug a keyring out of her bra, hastily unlocking the door and flinging it open. She stepped inside and Gentry began to follow her, but Mr. Tingles held out an arm, suddenly alarmed.

"Something's not right." His statement was followed by a pop that bounced off the greenhouse glass, through the trees and escaped into the morning air above them. Tingles realized as he heard another pop he'd hit the ground, and Gentry was next to him… still. He shook him violently and heard a soft groan. He was alive but clearly hurt.

Tingles grabbed Gentry's Glock, a weapon he hadn't used in years but felt natural in his hands. He'd fallen on his stomach, so had to roll over to look around and assess his surroundings. The glass in two panes of the greenhouse had been shattered, and shards surrounded him. He was careful not to touch any of it but quickly realized he'd rolled over into a pile of broken glass. As he looked everywhere for

Martha, he hoped none had punctured him. He carefully rose from the ground and looked down at Gentry. He could tell he was breathing but had certainly been hit. Tingles removed his cell phone from his pocket and dialed 911, notified them of their location and that a cop had been shot, and kneeled down to see if he could help while he waited on the emergency unit. Gentry had fallen on his back; if there was a bullet wound, it should have been on the front side of his body because that's the way he was facing the direction of the gunshots, however, Tingles didn't see a wound. Gentry was trying to speak, and Tingles leaned in to hear.

"Fi... Fi... nd her," he was saying.

"She can wait," Tingles said. Realistically, she couldn't have gotten far. In her condition, she couldn't have run. But... Why did she stop firing? If she'd wanted them dead and knew she couldn't get away, why would she give up the fight she'd started? It didn't make sense.

"Are you shot?" he asked Gentry hurriedly. Isaiah nodded yes, slowly, visibly in pain. "Where?"

"B... ba... c<u>k</u>," Gentry managed to say louder than before.

"Okay. Okay. You're going to be alright, Isaiah. Help is on the way. I need to roll you over and stop the bleeding." Tingles struggled to turn Isaiah. Gentry was over a foot taller than him and likely double his weight in pure muscle (all except that adorable dad-bod tummy Tingles found so endearing. It humanized Gentry to him and prevented him from being "another Greek Adonis homosexual cliche"). When he finally had him rolled over on his side, he immediately saw the gunshot wound. He tore the cream cape off his body he'd worn to counteract the cool August morning (that would undoubtedly yield to a hot day), balled it up, and placed it against the gunshot wound, pressing hard. There didn't seem to be a lot of blood coming from the wound, but since there wasn't a wound on the front of his torso, Tingles knew the bullet was still lodged in him.

With his hand pressing the sweater into Gentry's back, Tingles frantically looked around. He couldn't understand where Martha had gone. He also didn't understand how Isaiah had been shot in the back when… it hit him. Martha wasn't the shooter. He craned his neck until he could see enough of the greenhouse. One of the windowpanes had been shot out from the inside, but the other had been shot from the outside. Tingles followed the spray of glass with his eyes from the edge of the greenhouse until he saw a foot belonging to someone lying on the ground. He recognized the cat bedroom shoe.

Tingles heard sirens in the distance and knew help was close. He continued holding his sweater against Gentry's back and reassuring him he would be okay. As the sirens neared, Tingles continued to observe his surroundings. He looked off into the distance where he thought someone could have hidden… watched… and attacked. They were surrounded by woods, so anyplace was likely, really. Were they still watching? As he pondered and observed, one hand pressing the sweater into Isaiah's back, the other clutching his Glock, he was hyper-aware that another bullet could easily find its way to him. But the ambulance finally arrived, followed by three cop cars - Johnson, Carter, and an officer Tingles hadn't yet met.

As soon as the emergency responders arrived, Tingles bolted up and into the greenhouse where, as he suspected, Martha lay dead, a bullet through her skull. She held another shotgun in one hand. Tingles assumed she had guns stashed strategically around the property. He looked at the window Martha had shot through and remembered he'd only heard two shots. He was wrong, of course. There had to have been three - one that hit Gentry, one that hit Martha and the window of the greenhouse, and a final one *from* Martha. Everything had happened so quickly, though. It was then that Johnson appeared in the pane-less window of the greenhouse, looking worried. "They're taking Gentry to the hospital now. What the fuck happened here?"

"I can tell you what, but I don't know how or why yet," Tingles responded.

He was out of breath, shaken, and confused. His new friend and colleague had been shot, another woman dead, and his own life had been spared in a matter of seconds.

Tingles continued.

"We came here early to question Martha Raines. She pulled a shotgun on us, I talked her down and into talking with us, and she led us here. As soon as she walked in, we heard gunshots. Before I knew it, we were on the ground, Detective Gentry had been shot, Martha was dead, and I… I did everything I could to help him."

"He's going to be fine. That boy is a fighter. Right now, we need to figure out who the hell was trying to kill you both."

Tingles watched as Johnson had shifted from confused and angry at the scene he'd found to determined and mission-oriented in less than ten minutes. Johnson was, by all accounts, a country macho-man, but he was loyal to the law, the force, and especially Isaiah Gentry. For reasons Mr. Tingles couldn't explain, Johnson almost treated Isaiah like the son he never had. Now that the initial shock of him being shot had passed, Tingles knew Johnson was pissed, and his eyes were set on vengeance. Whoever had done this, Officer Johnson would see they would pay for it.

"The shots that hit Gentry and killed Martha came from the woods," Tingles said, pointing. "Martha shot out one window here. I'm not sure if she was defending us or herself, or if the gun went off when she was hit."

Tingles exited the door he'd come in - the same one Martha had unlocked and used right before all hell broke loose. He noted to Johnson on his way through that someone should obtain the keys and investigate the cottage where Martha lived.

"Whoever is behind this is our suspect for the murder of Brent DeCordts. I believe it is likely the woman we're looking for. We have made her nervous by arriving."

"Tingles, I don't understand how she knew you were coming here. And whoever she is, she's a hell of a shot. If she was shooting from all the way back there and not only hit Gentry but hit that woman" - he gestured to Martha's body - "then she didn't get lucky. She's got experience with a firearm."

"You're absolutely right about that. Good deduction!" Tingles responded. "That gives us something to work with. Criminals always get sloppy when they get scared. Let's investigate every female in the county with a gun permit. It's likely she doesn't have one, but this gives us a starting point. We also need to look through all of Ms. Raines' business documents, receipts, invoices… assuming she has any. Our suspect very likely purchased flowers from her and was afraid she'd talk."

"Think this Martha was involved with the DeCordts killing?" Johnson asked.

"I couldn't be sure, but my gut says no, or at least Martha is not who murdered Brent. It's too obvious. If she was, we're dealing with the dumbest criminals alive. The

Evita flower led us directly to her and I think that was the point. We need to know *why* our killer wanted us to find her."

"I don't understand, Tingles. If she killed the woman because she didn't want her to talk, then why would she plan for us to find her?"

"Because whatever she wants us to know is worth more to her than Martha's life."

CHAPTER TEN

Tingles and Johnson left Officer Carter in charge of the crime scene. By the time they left, the medical examiner and a slew of other officers had arrived so they could get to the hospital. Johnson's phone buzzed the entire twenty-minute drive from Martha's greenhouse to the Reidsville Hospital; people wanting to know if the rumblings of a police shootout were true and if Detective Gentry had actually been taken to the hospital. With each message he received Johnson muttered, "Oh, fuck off ya' nosey bastards!"

Tingles rode in the passenger seat, silent, wondering what he'd missed. Why hadn't he anticipated a trap? How did the suspect know they'd be there? Was there an insider feeding her information? He found that hard to believe because everyone was so close. Even Gentry, gay as he was and everyone knew it, was well-respected by the officers on the force. If they were homophobes, and undoubtedly some were, they held their positions, and Gentry's, in the highest regard. No, she had to have found out another way. It hit him.

"Goddamn Kimmie Flague," he muttered.

"What about her?" Johnson asked.

"Who gave Kimmie Flague a statement on the investigation yesterday?" Tingles asked.

"Umm…" Johnson thought. "Was supposed to be me and I got held up with a belligerent guy we were holding, so I think it got passed to Carter."

"Is there a record of what he told her?"

"I can find out. Usually, we just call so there probably isn't."

"I need to know exactly what he told her," Tingles said as they arrived at the hospital.

"I'll give him a call and tell him to get his ass down here as soon as they wrap up the crime scene."

Tingles nodded in agreement and the two hopped out of Johnson's patrol car and headed into the hospital. Once inside, the receptionist looked at Tingles with alarm. "Sir… are you okay?" he asked, and then yelled behind him, "We need a chair stat!" He was already around the counter when Tingles noticed what the man saw - he was covered in Gentry's blood. He hadn't noticed amid the chaos of the scene. He quickly explained they were there to see Detective

Gentry and that he had tried to control the blood loss while waiting for the ambulance. During his explanation, however, Mr. Tingles became weak and before he knew it was surrounded by blackness.

When he awoke, it was dark outside. He heard the slow beeping of the hospital equipment and felt like he'd been hit by a bus. For a moment he was confused; looking around at the unfamiliar drab walls, the small television attached to the wall playing reruns of *The Golden Girls*, and the smell of cleaning solutions were disconcerting. He hadn't noticed Johnson sitting next to him.

"How ya' feelin'?" he asked Tingles.

"Like shit," Tingles said, noticing how raspy his voice sounded. "How's Gentry?"

"He underwent surgery, but he's fine. They got the bullet out and it missed major arteries. He'll be good as new in a few weeks."

"Glad to hear it." Tingles' entire body relaxed at the news. He almost immediately felt energized and began fidgeting with the wires attached to him, muttering expletives as he tried to undo them.

"Whoa, whoa, whoa!" Johnson protested, standing. "What do you think you're doing, man?"

"I don't need to be here, officer," Tingles said

defiantly. "We need to figure out who shot Isaiah."

"Look, Tingles," Johnson said, placing a hand gently on his shoulder, the other on the arm he was using to try to pry off his cords. "Gentry is fine, you're fine, everyone is fine. But you both need to rest. I have officers hard at work – let them help."

Mr. Tingles gave in and lay back on his pillows. He knew Johnson was right, and when he conceded the point, he went back to feeling like shit. He thought back to the morning – their arrival at the greenhouse, how Martha had met them with hostility, how easily she'd been persuaded to talk, and how quickly the gunshots had rung through the woods. Maybe Martha had been warned they were coming and not to talk. The suspect had sat back and watched to make sure she didn't, and when Martha led them to the greenhouse after relinquishing her weapon to Tingles, she assumed Martha was giving her up, so she took her shot. Tingles considered the alternative, too. Martha was found dead with another shotgun. What if she was luring them into the greenhouse to kill them by making them think she was willing to talk? Maybe the suspect misunderstood what she was seeing and acted out of unnecessary caution. A third possibility was that Martha had no idea they were coming, no idea the suspect was involved in a murder and was just a mean old woman who got caught in the crosshairs of a nefarious murder plot. He decided the latter theory was the most likely but needed to know if anything had been found at the residence. Before he could inquire with Johnson the world had gone black again.

The following morning, early, Tingles awoke suddenly, confused. After several moments he remembered where he was and realized he hadn't gone to the restroom since the previous morning (that he remembered, anyhow). He fumbled until he found the remote control with a call button and pressed it vigorously. While waiting for a nurse he recalled Johnson had been there last evening, but he was gone now. The nurse came around the corner and greeted him with a smile. "Mornin' sunshine," she said cheerfully.

Must be the start of her shift, Tingles thought. *She's far too goddamn cheery to be coming off a twelve-hour stretch.*

"Good mornin'," Tingles croaked. "I need to use the bathroom," he said, getting straight to the point.

The nurse helped him up and to the restroom, got him back in bed, took his breakfast order, and supplied him with water and ginger ale. Tingles was feeling much better than he had last evening – almost back to normal, in fact. He knew he would need to rest and act like a sensible human being to get discharged, so he chose to bide his time, play nice, and get the hell out of there as soon as possible. There was work to be done. He looked around the room for his belongings. Locating the pants he'd been wearing he could see the outline of his phone in the pocket but couldn't reach it. He'd ask the nurse when she came back with breakfast. In the meantime, he grabbed the room phone and dialed for an operator. He wanted to speak with Isaiah.

"Mr. Gentry isn't awake yet," the woman on the other end of the line informed him after a few minutes. No, she didn't know when he'd be awake, but yes, she would let him know. He asked her for the number to the police station, instead.

"Donna? Oh good. I know it's ear…" he stopped and looked at the clock. It was just after 5am. *Shit*, early was an understatement. "…ly," he finished. "Is Officer Johnson there yet?"

"Yet?" Donna chuckled. "He ain't left since 9pm last night. Had to force him to eat a late dinner. He's in a tizzie over what happened!"

"We all are." Tingles replied.

"How's our boy?" Donna asked.

"I haven't been able to speak to him yet," Tingles answered.

"Well, that boy is a fighter," Donna began. "I just know he's going to be as good as ne…"

"Donna — " Tingles interrupted, forgoing his southern charm in the interest of getting an update on their case. "I don't mean to be rude, but may I speak with

Johnson, please?"

"Oh, sorry," Donna said. "I just get carried away. You got it, darlin'," she said, audibly offended, and placed the line on hold before Tingles could respond. A moment later Johnson was on the line.

"Tingles – mornin'! How the hell are you feeling?"

"Like shit," Tingles repeated. Johnson could hear his smirk as he said it. "Much better today, thank you. What do we have?"

"Nothing good. The handprints at the DeCordts home didn't give us a hit and no other prints were found at the home other than Brent's. We swept Martha's place and found a bunch of invoices for Gigi's Floral Fabulosity. I know the owner, so I gave her a visit last night. Turns out Martha was her sole source for rare flowers and – get this – her main buyer for the Evita flower is Mrs. DeCordts. What do you make of that?"

Johnson paused for a moment to catch his breath and sip on his eighth cup of coffee.

"Also, I've had officers question everyone we could find related to the original DeCordts case. Nothing new to speak of when compared to what we were told thirty-five years ago."

"Nothing good?" Tingles questioned dramatically. "It's gold, Johnson. The first time I stepped into Mrs. DeCordts home, I noticed a floral arrangement in her foyer that contained the Evita. Now we know our suspect was wearing that same flower in her hat the day the head was dropped off and was present at the home of the deceased. Now, either Mrs. DeCordts is involved, which I find unlikely due to her age and physical ability, or she has come into contact with our suspect. We need to question her again, but we have to be careful – she's already antsy. Have we located Joseph?"

"Nothing on Joseph. The boy has just disappeared. Want to question Mrs. DeCordts or have an officer do it?"

"He's got to be somewhere. Have an officer question everyone who knows him. Follow his spending receipts leading up to the closing of his bank accounts and question the people at the places he spent money. Request footage, too." He paused to catch his breath. "I'll take care of Mrs. DeCordts. We have history." As he finished, he heard a light knock on his door. "Keep me in the loop, Johnson, gotta go." He looked up as Kimmie Flague strolled through the door.

"Well good morning," she said brightly. "I heard on the police radio y'all were here – been waiting since yesterday to get a visit in." She invited herself to sit, threw one leg over the other, and rested her eyes squarely on Tingles' face. It was this moment that solidified his disdain for her. Kimmie had no boundaries and clearly lacked empathy. Here he and his partner were hospitalized, and she was nosing around for a goddamn story.

"How can I help you?" Tingles asked, not bothering to hide his annoyance with her presence.

"The question, Tingles, is how can *I* help *you?*"

"Get to the goddamn point, Kimmie. You may have noticed I'm in a hospital bed, so you'll forgive me if my patience is worn thin and I have no interest in this reenactment of *Whatever Happened to Baby Jane.*"

"I have information you need. I'm willing to give it to you in the interest of justice."

There's a big 'but' coming, Tingles thought.

"But," Kimmie continued as Tingles felt vindicated. "I need you to let me in this investigation. Full access."

"First of all, if you have information that could help with this investigation, and you withhold it I'll make sure you're arrested for obstruction of justice. Secondly, what you're asking is not my call, and the person who can make it will shut it down no sooner than you ask."

"That *is* unfortunate," Kimmie snapped with a slight hint of amusement in her voice. Whatever information she had must be good because she was quite confidently leveraging it to get what she wanted. "It's going to be very embarrassing for you and the department when a journalist breaks this case quicker than the detectives working it."

For a moment Tingles considered it and then decided he wouldn't allow himself to be manipulated.

Kimmie must have seen his look of consideration because she continued antagonizing him.

"Aren't you supposed to be, like, a brilliant detective? I have a lot less resources than you do, and I've already located Joseph DeCordts."

She had his attention, and she knew it. At that moment, however, before Tingles could settle into his embarrassment or get angry with her, Isaiah's voice cut in between them.

"Kimmie, you can tell us where he's at, or I'll have you arrested and taken in. After which you can rot in there."

Gentry looked like he probably felt like shit. His skin was pale, he had bags under his eyes, and he was slightly hunched over as he limped into the room. How he'd escaped his room, Tingles couldn't understand. What were the nurses doing that distracted them from a limping giant sneaking past them? Kimmie hadn't counted on Gentry showing up, and she shifted nervously in the chair she'd plopped on. Gentry noted her nervousness and took a seat on the edge of Tingles' bed.

Gentry's shirt was nowhere to be found, and he was bandaged from his belly button to his nipples. His "dad-bod belly" contrasted with his upper chest and arm muscles. Tingles, though not at all attracted to Gentry, couldn't help but notice he really was beautiful. He was an everyday man – not the type you'd see in a magazine, but the type you'd take home to mom and dad, proudly. Tingles felt a tinge of sadness that no one had ever taken him home to their parents. Maybe if he were forty years younger and his parents were still alive, he would. His dating days were a lifetime ago, though. He'd been single for over fifteen years and, save for a couple of drunken one-night stands, hadn't been intimate with a man in as much time. Gentry's voice broke the silence again.

"Kimmie, we've held up our end of the bargain we made. We've given you all the information we can without jeopardizing our investigation. You're a citizen, Kimmie. You don't get any journalistic immunity here. I'm asking you outright for information on the whereabouts of Joseph DeCordts in the interest of solving a murder. Now, you either tell me or pay the consequence for not."

"Oh, Isaiah, you're adorable," Kimmie said lightly. "I know my rights as a journalist, and I can guarantee you a judge would rule in favor of journalistic immunity if we ever took this to court. And to be sure, if you have me arrested, we will most certainly be going to court."

She stood now and paced the room in front of the hospital bed.

"Now, what I know so far is there's a rare flower called Evita that's been everywhere you have — in the box with the head, at Brent's, at Mrs. DeCordts, and at the greenhouse where you were attacked. I know you can't find

Joseph, haven't gotten any hits on prints from Brent's house, and can't I.D. your suspect. None of which was in the reports you sent me. Did I miss anything?"

"Plenty," Gentry said. "But that's the problem with collecting bits and pieces of information from… wherever the hell you're getting your information from."

"Carter," Tingles said. "How long have you been having… relations with him?"

His question was abrupt and settled into an awkward silence. Kimmie turned red – from anger or embarrassment he couldn't be sure, but Tingles would put his money on anger. She thought she'd out-smarted him, but Tingles had developed a feeling they were involved when she visited the station. Carter's gazes lingered longer than a passing glance. Gentry was impressed with Tingles' intuition. He'd also had a feeling they may be involved but hadn't spent enough time with either of them to be sure.

"That's none of your business. No matter where I got the information, I still know where Joseph is, and you still don't," she taunted.

Kimmie wasn't stupid, of that Tingles and Gentry were sure. She was holding her power of knowledge over their heads. What she didn't count on was the detectives' unwillingness to be manipulated or blackmailed.

"Well, Kimmie," Gentry said. "Looks like you're not interested in the public so much as your own agenda. Tell us where Joseph is or don't – we'll find out. You can be part of the solution or part of the problem, but again – if you obstruct this investigation, I *will* have you arrested." Just then a nurse walked in, red-faced, hands on her hips.

"Mr. Gentry, you have got to get back to your room!" she said sternly, but kindly. "I've been looking for you everywhere. You cannot heal if you don't rest."

She motioned for Isaiah to follow her back to his room as he rose from the corner of Tingles' bed and approached the doorway. He turned to Kimmie one last time before heading back to his room.

"Do what you gotta' do, Kimmie, but know this – we'll solve this case with or without your cooperation. Be a lot better for you if you cooperated." With that, he followed the nurse back to his room.

Tingles kept a gaze on Kimmie. He didn't trust her, but he wanted to keep her close. Throughout his career, he'd met a lot of people like her. Ambitious, power-hungry, and ego-driven were a combination which often led to chaos, as Kimmie had already proven in the few days Tingles had known her. He couldn't figure out what her end game was. Was she interested in climbing the ladder and making a name for herself? Or was it money she was after? Or, and Tingles thought this more likely, was she holding on to the grudge against Gentry? Tingles decided to address the elephant in the room.

"Miss Flague, what's your end goal?" Kimmie appeared to want to speak, but Tingles didn't slow down for her. "You know, sleeping with a police officer who can feed you information about cases doesn't make you a good journalist or a good investigator. It's cheap. It's a lazy way of investigating. Further, when the detective leading the case – the *only* detective in town – is your ex-boyfriend whom you outed because you were embarrassed you got dumped by a boy who likes boys, your efforts to obstruct his investigation just appear to be petty and vengeful. So, what's your endgame?"

Kimmie stepped closer to Tingles' bed. Her red cheeks gave away her rage at his comments, but otherwise, she was composed. She leaned in close to his ear and whispered:

"My end goal… is to show this town we don't need a couple of fairies to solve our crimes." She stood straight again, a bitchy expression across her face, and grabbed her purse off the chair. In a normal tone she said, "I suppose we're going to both investigate on our own terms, huh? See who can solve this thing first?"

"It isn't a competition, Kimmie," Tingles said. "There can be no competition between players who are unwilling to compete."

"You're right about that, Tingles," Kimmie responded. "There is no competition. Just two people who want to find a killer."

Kimmie stared at him for a few moments before turning towards the door.

"Kimmie," Tingles continued, and she turned back around to face him. Without speaking she shifted her weight onto one hip, wrist resting on it, with a "what do you want?" expression.

"You need to make amends with Isaiah. You stole his opportunity to tell his family about his identity; you kept him from figuring himself out on his own timeline. You may think of him as a *fairy*, but he's a human being and he's a good man. He didn't deserve what you did to him, and he is still paying the price. Being gay in the south ain't for sissies, honey, I'll tell you that." As he continued, his voice lowered and Kimmie noted a sense of sadness. "Many don't make it out alive because of people like you. You have a choice to make about the kind of person you want to be. I hope you'll make the right decision."

Kimmie had lingered in the doorway a few more moments before turning and walking away in silence. Tingles had hit a nerve. As she walked down the hallway to the elevator, she considered his words. She didn't owe Isaiah a goddamn thing. He'd hurt her, embarrassed her even. Everyone in the school found out she'd been dating a sissy. Her own love life suffered because of it, and people even bullied her saying if she'd touched or kissed him, she would end up a dyke. Here they were, a decade later and she wasn't gay – but he still was. Somehow, his being back in town reflected poorly on her. She was trying to prove herself as much as he was. She'd paid consequences for him being a faggot, too, and she was determined to embarrass him the way he'd embarrassed her – by showing the town he wasn't a skilled detective, but the sissy they'd always thought him to be. Carter had given her enough information to get started, and she did know where Joseph was. She planned to question him and the owner of Gigi's Floral Fabulosity. She had a hunch Joseph knew something about the case, just like she was sure Mrs. DeCordts did. After all, Joseph was living in her home.

CHAPTER ELEVEN

Mr. Tingles was released from the hospital three days later. He hadn't been struck by any bullets, but the fall he took with Gentry had taken a heavy toll on his body. He went straight to the Reidsville Inn to shower and dress. He was relieved to be rid of the hideous nightgown the hospital had forced him to wear and back into something that was more his style. He decided on a champagne-colored suit, trimmed in black with — as always — a matching fedora with an array of feathers on the side. He made his way to the Reidsville Police Department where he'd arranged to meet Johnson. The two caught up on the few developments they'd only discussed by phone and Tingles made him aware of what they'd discovered from Kimmie, including her relationship with Officer Carter. Johnson became incensed to learn Carter had been feeding her information. Tingles needed to be sure, though, that Carter was their mole. The biggest mistake they could make was to assume he was the one feeding her information, with no proof. Besides, Kimmie had looked smug when they exposed her relationship with Carter and brushed it off. Either she didn't give a damn about him, or they had gotten it wrong that Carter was the one feeding her intel. Tingles devised a plan to give Carter a statement for Kimmie which contained false information. If she bit, then they'd know it was Carter. This was, of course, assuming she hadn't told Carter they were on to them. Tingles thought that was unlikely. If Carter knew they suspected him of feeding information to Kimmie, then he'd assume he'd be in trouble and be much more careful, perhaps even stop sharing. He'd be right, of course, to be concerned about being disciplined. Tingles knew he'd lose his job, so he wanted to use him while he could but prevent him from feeding any more information to Kimmie if he was, in fact, guilty of it.

With Johnson in the conference room, Tingles mapped out what they'd learned since the last time they met.

- ❖ Martha Raines was an expert in growing rare flowers.
- ❖ Her primary customer was Gigi's Floral Fabulosity.
- ❖ Therefore, their suspect had to have gotten the Evita flowers from Martha or Gigi's.
- ❖ Mrs. DeCordts was Gigi's main customer for the

Evita.

❖ Joseph DeCordts was still missing to them, but apparently Kimmie had knowledge of his whereabouts – they would put a tail on her. If she knew where to find him, then she'd lead them right to him.

"Am I missing anything?" Tingles asked.

"Nothin' I can think of," Johnson said. "Want me to drive you over to Gigi's?"

"That'd be lovely. Thank you, officer."

The two gathered their things and headed towards the door. Johnson stopped in the doorway and looked down at Tingles. "Y'know I worried about ya'... when you collapsed, y'know?"

Tingles cocked his head a little, surprised by Johnson's candor. Johnson was a "macho-man"; Tingles was completely caught off guard to hear him express something that left him so vulnerable. Further, he was shocked to hear him say something that made Tingles question whether he was flirting with him. He'd worried about Tingles... why would he worry? They hardly knew each other. The tension between them grew in the moments following Johnson's words. For the first time since he'd met Johnson, Tingles noticed he was an attractive man. Tall, and surprisingly built for a man of his age, Johnson also had jet black hair with a light peppering of gray and no signs of thinning – a selling point for most men over forty, and especially over fifty. He was also a kind man, as evidenced by his concern for Mr. Tingles. He knew, however, all too well, the dangers of allowing oneself to fall for a straight man. He didn't want to allow himself the luxury of puppy-love for a man he was probably only imagining was flirting with him.

"Well…." Tingles said, airily. "I appreciate that, Officer. I'm glad to have made a full recovery."

"Yeah," Johnson said, looking Tingles in the eyes. And then, softer, he said, "I'm glad, too."

Tingles and Johnson arrived at Gigi's Floral Fabulosity a few minutes before five. As they walked in, they heard a woman's voice say, "We're closin' up, folks. Sorry." A young blonde woman came around the corner. "Can I help you?" she asked.

"Yes ma'am," Tingles said, taking a step towards the woman. "My name is Detective Tingles, and this is Officer Johnson. We're investigating a homicide that has led us to this quaint shop."

Quaint was one word to describe the shop. It was small and chock-full of flowers. The walls were lined with coolers that contained already assembled floral arrangements. There was a curtain they could see led to a walk-in cooler. Through a gap in the curtain Tingles spotted what looked like *seemannia nematanthodes.*

"Led you to us?" the woman replied, unsure whether to be amused or insulted.

"Yes, ma'am," Tingles said. "Are you the owner of this establishment?"

"No, I just work here," she replied. "I'm Christina."

"Nice to meet you, Christina. I just have a few questions for you. I understand you sell a flower called *seemannia nematanthodes.* Is that correct?"

Christina looked at him with a confused expression. She obviously had never heard of *seemannia nematanthodes.*

"Don't know what that is," she replied.

"It's also referred to as 'Evita.' Perhaps you've heard of that?" Tingles responded.

"Ahhhh." Christina recognized Evita. "Mrs. DeCordts' flower.".

"That's an interesting thing to say," Tingles noted. "Is she the *only* person who buys the flower?"

"Yes, sir. She's the only reason we carry it. Of course, with what happened to Miss Martha I guess she'll be out of luck."

"Yes, I suppose she will be," Tingles said. "Is Martha the only person you acquired Evita from? No other suppliers carry it?"

"Yep. She's the only one within a hundred miles who

grows it. Well… the only one who *did*."

"How often does Mrs. DeCordts purchase flowers from you all?"

"She has a standing weekly order. The Evita is part of it. Every Monday she or her son comes in to pick them up."

"You said her son?" Johnson said, speaking for the first time and his bombastic voice took Christina by surprise. Tingles noted the surprise in Johnson's voice which he was also feeling.

"Yes, sir. Cheryl or Joseph is here every Monday at 6am to pick up their orders. Florist usually comes in Sunday afternoon to prepare their arrangements and have them fresh."

"Why so early?" Johnson inquired.

"So no one sees them," Tingles said, then, looking at Christina, "Right?"

"Dunno," Christina said. "All she's said is they like to avoid the crowds."

"You're sure it's Joseph?" Johnson asked.

"Well, Brent's dead, ain't he?" Christina asked. "Joseph is the only living twin, and he was just here this past Monday."

"Any idea where he's living? Do you all keep addresses for your customers?"

"Well, since the flowers are for Mrs. DeCordts, we

have hers on file. Nothing for him."

"Thank you, Christina. We'll call you if we have more questions."

Tingles and Johnson left the floral shop with an unspoken, mutual understanding they were headed to Mrs. DeCordts' home. As they approached Johnson's patrol car, Tingles noticed him making his way to the passenger side door. He opened it and gestured for Tingles to climb in.

Okay. Tingles thought. *He's definitely flirting with me.*

Johnson closed the door behind Tingles and got in, cranked the engine, and drove them over to Mrs. DeCordts home. On the way, Tingles called the hospital to speak with Gentry, who was sleeping. The nurse informed him he had been behaving badly – getting out of bed and roaming the halls, making phone calls, detaching his IVs, etc. – if he could please tell him to behave they'd be so appreciative. Tingles said he would, and bid the nurse farewell. He wasn't surprised Gentry couldn't sit still. Many queer people, especially those who'd had traumatic upbringings, such as Gentry (and Tingles, for that matter), had a hard time acting in their own best interests. Much of their lives were spent in fight or flight mode and choosing their own health and well-being wasn't always uppermost in their minds. Tingles felt a tinge of sadness fall over him at the thought of Gentry not knowing he was good enough or valuable enough to take care of himself. He'd have a talk with him after they left Mrs.

DeCordts' home. Johnson and Donna weren't the only people who were protective over Gentry. Tingles had come to care for the young man in the short time he'd known him, and he had no problem admitting it was because Gentry was a young queer man who reminded him of himself. "We take care of our own," he'd said over and over throughout his life.

The short car ride with Johnson was mostly quiet. Tingles noticed himself feeling nervous – giddy, in fact. Having noticed Johnson's increased attention on him and allowing himself the luxury of finding the man attractive, Tingles was feeling something he hadn't felt in years. His heart beat faster when he was around Johnson, and he was fighting the urge to grab him and kiss him. How had it happened in a single day? Maybe he only felt this way because he hadn't received any attention from a man in so long. Or maybe, Tingles thought…. *Shit. I have a crush.* This was disastrous. Tingles wasn't a teenager; he was a man in his sixties. As his mother had often said, he'd been "rode hard and put up wet" by life and had given up on finding the next love of his life over a decade ago. Like most feelings that made him feel vulnerable, Tingles filed his crush on Johnson away. He'd deal with it later – or not.

They arrived at Mrs. DeCordts' home a little after 6pm. The southern August heat battered the two men as they approached her front door again. Tingles raised a hand to knock on the door, but it opened before his knuckles found it. Standing in front of him was not Mrs. DeCordts, but Kimmie Flague. Perhaps she was being genuine when she said she knew where Joseph was. Tingles would take no chances, however, and wouldn't let on he knew Joseph had been seen picking up flowers for his mother on Mondays. Immediately, he questioned why Kimmie would be there if she didn't also suspect Joseph was there. Perhaps just to question Mrs. DeCordts.

"Well, Detective Tingles and Deputy Fife. Howdy!" Kimmie said energetically as if she liked them, and they didn't despise her. "To what do we owe the pleasure?" By this time Mrs. DeCordts had arrived next to Kimmie.

"Kimmie, please," Mrs. DeCordts snipped, stepping in front of her. Kimmie looked offended and rolled her eyes. "What do you want now?" Mrs. DeCordts barked at Tingles and Johnson. "I'm really quite busy."

"We have some developments in the case and have a few follow up questions for you," Tingles said.

"Can it wait?" Mrs. DeCordts replied sharply. Tingles could tell she was shutting down. This may be their last opportunity to get any useful information from the old battle ax.

"I'm afraid not, ma'am." Johnson had stepped up and taken over the conversation. Tingles, while assertive when necessary, was more naturally a charmer who possessed much more patience than him. Tingles noted that

Johnson had run out of his patience for the day and was adamant Mrs. DeCordts was going to cooperate. This act of macho-ism – the insistence they had to question her now, the baritone in his voice, his tall and imposing stature – sent chills through Tingles who found himself having to physically refrain from melting into the porch.

"This matter is of grave importance and pertains to the murder of your son. So, we'd like to come in, and we'd like Ms. Flague to leave."

"Hmph," Mrs. DeCordts grunted, followed by a deep sigh. "Come in, I guess," she snapped. "But Kimmie stays – I've allowed her full access to me throughout the course of this investigation. Anything I know, she knows. I won't have this police department ruining me the way they ruined my late husband." With that, Mrs. DeCordts cut her eyes at Mr. Tingles as she always did when mentioning her late husband. "Kimmie is here to ensure that doesn't happen, and I've retained a lawyer who is ready to destroy you if you try. Understand?"

Shit, Tingles thought. Kimmie Flague had wiggled her way to a front-row seat in this investigation. She knew Mrs. DeCordts would be provided information since her son was the victim. Tingles looked over at Johnson and, once he collected his heart from his stomach, caught his gaze and they both understood they needed to be careful about what they said and asked. Tingles spoke on their behalf:

"Yes ma'am. We understand, and we appreciate your cooperation. May we come in?"

Mrs. DeCordts flung open the door fully and stood aside to allow the gentlemen inside. Like the last time, Tingles led the way to the sitting room and, once they arrived, gestured to Johnson where he could sit. Mrs. DeCordts and Kimmie trailed close behind, their high heels clacking against the wood floors like gunshots. Tingles felt anxious as the sound triggered the very recent memory of actual gunshots. It wasn't the first time he'd been in a situation like the one he'd experienced a few days prior, and may not be the last, but the memories were stubborn, and physiological responses to sounds like high heels on hardwood floors were unavoidable. Tingles had noticed on his way through the hall Mrs. DeCordts was displaying an arrangement of Evita flowers just like she had the past two times he'd been there. He knew this would be one of the last times he saw the arrangement due to Martha's death. Now that everyone was situated in the sitting room, Mr. Tingles began:

"Mrs. DeCordts, I'll be direct so as not to waste your time. It has come to our attention that you have likely had contact with your son Joseph – regular contact with him. Is that true?"

"Yes. Is that a crime?"

"Seeing your son is not, Cheryl," Tingles said, the use

of her first name catching her off guard. "Lying to the police about it is, though. Why did he go off the radar?"

Before she had a chance to respond, Johnson cut in saying, "Mrs. DeCordts, cooperate now and answer our questions, and we'll overlook your lying to us before. Understand?"

Without acknowledging the interruption, Mrs. DeCordts continued: "Right after Paul died, we learned someone was stalking him. Sending him crazy letters to his apartment, sitting in a car outside his building, even calling his office, and just… breathing into the phone. He went to the cops," she said, looking over at Johnson. "They told him without something concrete they couldn't do anything. So, he gave up his apartment, closed all his bank accounts, credit cards, and anything else that had his name on it, and came to live here. About the only thing he leaves for is to pick up flowers for me on Monday mornings and the occasional doctor's appointment. Otherwise, he works from home, eats, sleeps, and repeats."

"Why didn't you tell us?" Johnson asked. Tingles liked his assertiveness.

"I told you he was being stalked, and your force didn't do anything about it. Given our history with the police in this town, you can understand that we don't have much faith in you. I thought he was safer in hiding."

"Do you have any idea who was stalking him?"

Tingles asked.

"No. A woman, I'm certain."

"Why?" Johnson asked.

"The sighs on the phone when she called him were… feminine," Mrs. DeCordts said. "She called over and over."

"She called him or you?" Tingles asked. He was starting to get the impression the stalker was targeting Mrs. DeCordts, too.

"Both," she replied. "I assumed she was calling for him, but it was alarming, nonetheless."

"Did she ever say anything?" Johnson asked.

"No. Only breathed into the phone."

"Mrs. DeCordts, I can understand your past experience with the police has been… unpleasant," Johnson began, "but, with all due respect, you didn't think a woman stalking your son – and possibly you – was important information to give us when you discovered your son had been murdered?"

Officer Johnson's question lingered. Kimmie's gaze had drifted to the floor while Mrs. DeCordts just looked dazed. Finally, Mrs. DeCordts breathed heavily and looked up at Johnson.

"Yes. It occurred to me that whoever murdered Brent could be the person stalking hi… us. We have such little confidence in your force, however, we believed we would be better off handling this ourselves."

"*You* thought we would be better off," an unfamiliar voice chimed in.

All four parties turned to the doorway where a tall, slender, imposing man stood. His hair was jet black and cascaded down to his shoulders. His skin was pale, his eyes dark, and his clothes black. Tingles thought he looked like a goth kid who'd grown up to be a goth professional. Perhaps the type of kid who hadn't healed from a turbulent past but was smart enough to know he had to work for a living. As Tingles took in the man's appearance, he suddenly realized he was looking at...

"Detectives. Meet my son, Joseph."

CHAPTER TWELVE

Joseph was a quiet young man but looked intimidating. The darkness of his hair and clothes, contrasted by the paleness of his skin, made him look like a character from an Anne Rice novel. The softness of his voice and calmness of his demeanor, however, was more akin to Mister Rogers. Mr. Tingles was astounded at how much he'd changed since he was twelve years old while simultaneously looking the same. He had the same demeanor as he'd shown when Tingles interviewed him thirty years earlier, and his eyes showed the same emptiness, but he was certainly older. The bags under his eyes made him appear ghostly.

Tingles observed Joseph's every move – the way he walked, how he sat, the way he didn't look his mother in the eyes (he barely looked at her at all), and especially the way he avoided Kimmie. Tingles thought the young man was a bit of a mystery himself. He had the distinct impression Joseph was bitter, perhaps emotionally unstable, and, at the very least had a complicated relationship with his mother. This was the type of behavior common in adults who had not healed from traumatic childhood experiences. What had he endured? Why was his relationship with his mother so damaged? What was this entire fucking family hiding?

The four of them sat for several moments in silence, Joseph's presence having cast a dark cloud over the conversation. Tingles wanted to ask him questions but knew with his mother there, he may not answer them honestly, or at all. He decided to stick with the line of questioning he'd been aiming at Mrs. DeCordts.

"Joseph, since you've joined us, is there anything you can tell us about the stalker?"

"Not much," he said softly but defiantly, like a teenager being stubborn for the sake of being stubborn. Then he added, "I mean I never saw her."

"Were the phone calls all you experienced? How can you be sure you were being stalked?" Tingles asked.

He grunted – something between a chuckle and a snort. "You sound like the police when I reported it. I saw the same car following me from a distance every day for weeks. It was parked outside my apartment building for several nights. The phone calls went on for weeks – my cell, my job, here. A few times I'd swear I saw someone standing in the window down at Brent's, but it was always dark, and I couldn't be sure. Got to a point where we hadn't heard from him, anyway, after he came in here begging for money. Thought he might just have a friend over. Just freaked me out seeing a figure in that window every night. Told all of this to your guys at the station and they said it wasn't enough to investigate. 'Maybe it was a coincidence,' they said."

Officer Johnson shifted in his chair. He didn't like hearing someone criticize his colleagues, but he recognized the harm their negligence had caused. Perhaps if whoever he'd spoken to had taken him seriously Brent would be alive. Who could tell? Tingles, on the other hand, latched onto one part of Joseph's story immediately.

"You say you thought you saw someone standing in Brent's window? Do you have any vague recollection of what the person looked like? Gender, age, clothes? Anything at all that could help?" Tingles asked.

"All I could see was whoever it was looked small. Along with the feminine-sounding breathing, I deduced that whoever the person in the window was must be the person making the phone calls, therefore, a woman. I could be wrong, though."

"When's the last time you saw or heard from this person?" Johnson asked.

"Haven't received any calls in a week or so. The last time I left the house was to pick up flowers for mama. I always go early – less traffic and less chance of being seen. I didn't see her then. I've stayed clear of the hallway window, too."

"Interesting," Tingles said.

"Joseph, we'd also like to ask you questions about the murder of Darren Southern. Would you be will…" Johnson began.

"We're done here," Mrs. DeCordts interjected. "How dare you?" she hissed at Johnson. "Your police force and this sissy faggot framed my husband for murder, ignored my son's plea for help, and now my other son is dead, and you have the nerve…"

"MA'AM," Johnson said loudly. It wasn't quite a yell, but he wasn't calm.

Mrs. DeCordts cowered at the volume, though, and Johnson realized he'd been louder than he intended. He didn't bother apologizing, but he lowered his voice and said sternly:

"You're allowed to be upset, but if you call Detective Tingles another derogatory name, you'll regret it. Now, we have reason to believe the murder of Darren Southern is connected to your son's murder and we *will* be asking questions of you and your son about it. Understood?"

"Not without our lawyer, you won't," Mrs. DeCordts snapped at him. "Now get the fuck out of my house!"

Kimmie giggled lightly under her breath. Not only had she been retained by Mrs. DeCordts to help write her narrative for the public, but Kimmie had secured a front-row seat to their investigation. There was no way they could question the DeCordts' without her there which meant information such as the relation to the Southern murder was bound to fall in her lap. It didn't matter now, Tingles thought. She'd known before them where Joseph was, and she now knew they believed there was a connection to a cold case. They would just have to move forward the best they could and be careful of her involvement. Now their biggest challenge was making sure she didn't get in their way.

Tingles and Johnson lifted themselves out of their chairs and headed out the way they'd come. Joseph, Mrs. DeCordts, and Kimmie sat silently while they turned the corner of the doorway and headed to the front door. Tingles pulled a card out of the breast pocket of his blazer and laid it on the table next to the door. He wasn't sure who he was leaving it for, but he tapped it with his index finger as he turned to walk through the door Johnson held open for him. His heart fell to his stomach again as he glided through towards the patrol car.

When Tingles and Johnson arrived back at the station, they were shocked to find Detective Gentry at his desk. Tingles had protested his return to work and Johnson had chastised him for leaving the hospital so soon. The two were like the parents Gentry wished he'd had. Shortly after, Donna had lectured him, too, though she'd brought him coffee and sweets and was, therefore, hard to take seriously. Gentry explained to them the wound was not severe; the bullet hadn't made it far, its extraction went smoothly, and other than a little pain he was fine. Most of his issues had been due to exhaustion. His two colleagues weren't buying it and convinced him that if he was going to be back at work, he would take it easy – if not for his own sake, for theirs.

Once the debates over Gentry's well-being and capability to be at work concluded they got to work filling him in on everything they'd learned. How Martha had shot through one pane of glass but the other shot came from the woods. How Mrs. DeCordts was the only person in town who bought the Evita flower from Gigi's Floral Fabulosity. That Joseph wasn't *missing* but hiding at his mother's because of a stalker, and finally that Kimmie Flague had been hired by Mrs. DeCordts as some kind of investigative journalist responsible for writing her story and protecting her image from the Reidsville Police Department.

Gentry sat with the new information for several minutes. Tingles and Johnson exchanged glances that questioned Gentry's train of thought. Finally, Gentry spoke: "So, we know our suspect was in Brent's home. We know the home wasn't lived in due to the layers of dust, but someone was there recently because of the handprint in the dust. We also found another Evita in the home. So, it sounds like Brent was either dead longer than we thought, or she had him held captive."

"I have a theory," Tingles said. "But to prove it, I need to dig more into the Southern murder files."

"What are you thinking, Tingles?" Gentry asked.

"That whoever our suspect is knows who murdered Darren Southern and is acting out a plan of vengeance. It's the only thing that makes sense."

"But who?" Johnson asked. "The only person I can think of is the wife who's missing. The daughter was only three. Ain't no way she'd remember something she saw when she was three."

"I'm not sure," Tingles said, feeling a little defeated, slinking down into his chair. "It's a gut feeling, I just don't have the evidence to prove it – *just like 30 years ago.*"

It was true Tingles was feeling like he had three decades ago. He hadn't been able to catch a killer then and was starting to feel like he wouldn't this time. He'd only been there for a little more than two weeks but felt like he, Gentry, and Johnson were getting nowhere. Again, they had more questions than answers, no viable suspects, and people who refused to answer their questions. All Tingles needed was one key piece of information or evidence that would set the rest of the investigation into motion. What was he missing in their mess of information? A phone ringer interrupted his train of thought. He snapped out of his daze and looked around trying to find the source of the ringing until Johnson pointed out it was his own phone. He pulled it out of his pocket and swiped the button to accept the call.

"Detective Tingles," he said. Johnson and Gentry watched his expression change as whoever was at the other end spoke. "Yes, I can meet you. Where?" A moment passed. "Fine. We'll see you soon."

Johnson and Gentry looked at Tingles with anticipation until he said, "Joseph DeCordts would like to meet with us and make a statement."

CHAPTER THIRTEEN

Joseph requested to meet in an abandoned field next to an old church on the outskirts of town. He'd be waiting for them, he said. Johnson was the first to point out that last time Gentry and Tingles had ventured into a rural spot they'd ended up in the hospital. He insisted Gentry stay behind.

"Over my dead body!" Gentry had said.

"Have another situation like the other morning and it will be," Johnson had retorted, but ultimately lost the argument.

The trio decided they'd all go, armed, and have a couple of patrol cars follow them and post within watching distance. If they had eyes around the field, then it was less likely a shooter would try anything. Tingles no longer thought Joseph was involved in the disappearance of his brother, but the forthcoming interview would reveal more to him, he thought. One thing Tingles was sure of was the DeCordts family was hiding something – a feeling he'd had since 1989.

The trio set out at 8:30pm for their 9pm rendezvous with Joseph. Tingles shivered at the thought of meeting such a creepy person in the darkness of a rural field. He thought maybe he should be more concerned about Joseph being a vampire than a murderer, though truth be told he was most concerned about ruining his suede shoes. The ride to the outskirts of town was beautiful at sunset. They zoomed past tobacco fields laid out on either side of them like oceans, an orange tinge glowing over them which made them appear on fire. As the sun continued to set, Tingles noticed fireflies or, as he called them, "lightnin' bugs," starting a show of lights against the darkness settling in on them. He loved watching the lightnin' bugs. He often sat on his porch in Winston Salem, a glass of sweet tea or lemonade in his hand, and watched them for hours. They reminded him of a simpler time in his life before he knew he was gay or what gay meant before he'd embarked on a career of catching criminals, and before he'd seen so much death. They brought him comfort.

The radio played softly in Gentry's SUV - not only had he insisted on going but driving, as well. Tingles didn't know if the station was random or one Gentry chose, but he enjoyed the classic country coming from the speakers. Loretta Lynn, Patsy Cline, Dolly Parton… all of his favorites. Currently "Coal Miner's Daughter" played and reminded him of his mother. She'd been a beacon of strength for most of his life. Much like Loretta Lynn she'd survived a poor upbringing, an abusive marriage, and four miscarriages before finally having a baby boy. He watched her work her ass off in a time when it was hard for a single woman to work at all. She managed to take care of them, though.

His father came and went throughout his life, his mother welcomed him back only when times were particularly tough. Then, when she found out Tingles was gay, she changed. She kicked him out of her home – no faggot would live with her and disrespect the Lord. He spoke to her a handful of times after that, never spoke to his father again, and wasn't notified either had died. He found out when he went back to his hometown for a case and ran into an old family friend. "I was so sorry to hear about your parents," they'd said. They'd gotten back together for the umpteenth time and died in a car accident. Tingles never quite recovered from the downfall of his relationship with his mother who had taught him so many valuable lessons, but he'd found ways to cope. He was empathetic towards Isaiah and even Joseph; he knew how it felt to have a turbulent relationship with your mother.

Lost in thought, Tingles hadn't noticed they were approaching a church and a large field until Johnson spoke. "Here we are," he said. The three of them saw a car was already parked in the field. The patrol cars they'd assigned to follow them and keep watch took their places. They weren't trying to be discreet – they wanted Joseph to know that if he was up to something, it was something he wouldn't get away with. Gentry drove the SUV through the grass and parked in front of him, the fronts of their vehicles facing one another.

Joseph got out of his silver 2023 Nissan Rogue and held his palms out to his sides to convey to the trio he didn't have a weapon. Johnson made a show of letting Joseph know the three of them *were* armed. Joseph dropped his hands and looked at them for a moment before he spoke. He seemed nervous.

"Look, I want to tell you guys something I think you need to know. Could be relevant to your investigation. But I need to know that you won't ever tell my mother where you got this information."

"If that is possible, then you have our word," Tingles said.

"Not good enough," Joseph responded. "I need your word now."

"You have it," Gentry said. Tingles wanted to protest. How could they make a promise before they knew what he had to say? Joseph looked at Tingles and Johnson as if asking them to promise, too. If they didn't, they would never know what he had to say.

"I promise," Tingles said.

"You have my word," Johnson echoed.

Joseph hesitated before settling into a feeling of relief. He leaned back against the 2023 Rogue, pulled out a pack of Camel Crush menthol cigarettes, placed one between his lips and lit it. He took a long drag and inhaled, finally releasing the smoke slowly.

"I don't really know how to say it – the secret I've been hiding for over thirty years could ruin my mother and, although he's dead, Brent's reputation. Maybe… Maybe there's nothing to it and I'm overreacting. All I know is my twin brother is dead, and my mother isn't cooperating with law enforcement at all. Her hiring Kimmie Flague as a private investigator or investigative journalist is a joke, too. My mother would never tell Kimmie the things she really needs to know, making it impossible for her to solve Brent's murder. Of course, the relinquishing of this information all hinges on my understanding that you believe Brent's death was related to Darren Southern's. So, I felt compelled to help even if it does defame my family further."

Joseph realized he'd just been rambling, the three law enforcement officials staring at him with blank expressions.

"You said Brent's death could be connected to Darren Southern's?" He said it more like a question and spoke slowly, cautiously.

Tingles took a step forward. The three of them knew at that point this conversation was for him.

"We do believe so, yes," Tingles said.

"Do you remember questioning us?" Joseph asked, followed by another drag of his Camel.

"Like it was yesterday," Tingles responded. The sun had finally set and he noticed they were surrounded by lightnin' bugs, lighting up the now-dark field as they conversed.

"Well, the story we told… it wasn't true," Joseph said quietly, the latter half of the sentence trailing off, lost in the summer air. And then, "Everyone wasn't home… all night."

"Who wasn't home?" Tingles asked. There was urgency in his voice – he was about to get information on one of three unsolved cases from his career, and the excitement was palpable.

"My mother. And Brent. They were gone for a few hours that evening. When they came home my mom brought us all to the living room and told us what to say when the cops asked. Even made us rehearse it."

"Where were they? Do you know?" Tingles asked.

"I have no idea," Joseph answered. "Just that they weren't home, and they made us lie about it. I've never forgiven myself, and now Brent is dead and maybe it's connected. I just… thought you should know."

Joseph's voice had trailed off as if he was keeping himself from crying. Tingles could tell he felt responsible for his brother's death.

"Did Brent sneak out? Or did he go somewhere with your mother?" Tingles asked

"He snuck out around eight. I remember because I had been working on homework and didn't realize how late it was. We were supposed to play a video game together and I went to his room to tell him we'd have to wait until the next night to play because I still had so much to get done. When

I opened his bedroom door his window was open, and he was dressed all in black. There was a rope hanging from his window and he looked like he was about to throw a leg over the windowsill. I asked him what he was doing, and he said he had to do something. Wouldn't tell me what. A while later the phone rang, and I heard my mom from the other room saying she'd be there as soon as she could. This was sometime after 10pm. She was quiet when she walked down the hallway. I was still working on homework, but I think she thought I was asleep. I peeked out my window when I heard the garage door open and saw her car back out. About an hour later she pulled back in with Brent in the car."

"You did the right thing, young man. We can help protect you during this investigation, if you'd like?"

"No. I'll be okay. Not many people know where I am, so I feel safe."

"I do have a couple of more questions. Do you think your mother killed Darren Southern?"

"I don't know. There was a rumor back then that my mom and Darren were having an affair. I heard her arguing with my dad about it once. Truthfully, if he hadn't been home with me that night, I'd think he did it. But he couldn't have."

"You're quite sure your father never left, too?"

"Yes. Like I said, I was up. I heard him all night in his office working. Typing away on that goddamn typewriter. Hate the sound of those things."

"Do you think Brent or your mother were capable of killing Darren?"

Joseph chuckled a little, choking on the smoke he'd just inhaled. "Brent? Unlikely," he said. "He was a wimp. I can't imagine him murdering someone, but… he did have anger issues. But hell, we were only twelve, detective."

"Younger people have done much worse."

"I guess so," Joseph replied, clearly not convinced his brother was capable of murder. "My mother is a cold-hearted bitch, but I don't think she could kill anyone either. She can barely squash a spider without getting nauseous."

Joseph shifted his weight nervously, though relieved to have gotten this off his chest. Tingles could tell he was being truthful he didn't know if his mother had killed Darren Southern and he also didn't think Brent could have done it, but this new order of events intrigued him. He hoped he and Gentry could do something with the information he gave them.

"Look, I don't know if what I told you will help. It might be nothing. My family has always been fucked up, and I despise my mother – my only living relative left. But I don't want my legacy to be hiding information that could have caught a killer. Maybe two."

"Thank you, Joseph," Tingles said. He meant it.

CHAPTER FOURTEEN

Tingles had been energized by the conversation with Joseph DeCordts. He didn't know how yet, but he was sure this was the piece of information he'd waited over thirty years to receive. This would crack the Darren Southern case *and* the Brent DeCordts case – he just knew it. He ran the details in his mind. Brent left the DeCordts' home around 8:30pm, returning somewhere around 11pm with Mrs. DeCordts. Cheryl had left home around 10pm after receiving a phone call. Since she'd returned with Brent, it only made sense he was the one who'd called. So, where had he been? Maybe he'd only been drunk. But why would Mrs. DeCordts tell the entire family to lie? That was the piece which deconstructed every other scenario. Mrs. DeCordts had instructed her entire family to lie about them all being home, eating dinner, watching television, and going to bed. *Why?* Tingles told Gentry and

Johnson he'd need to see all of the original case files himself. He wanted to sift through every document, photo, and scrap of paper in the box. With this new information, he may be able to identify some gaps in their investigation to follow up on.

"I can help you out with that," Johnson had offered. "If, uh… y'know… you want help with it."

"I'd like that," Tingles had responded.

Gentry decided to drop them off and head home. He hadn't had a good night's sleep in days and probably wouldn't get one tonight, but at least he'd be in his own bed. He made his way to Vestel Drive and arrived home close to eleven. His motion sensor porch light, a floodlight which illuminated his entire yard, was activated when he pulled into his driveway, and he saw a figure on his porch. "Who the fuck?" he mumbled to himself. He threw the SUV in park and got out, a hand on his Glock. As he approached his own porch he said, "May I help y…" and stopped short when he finally recognized the woman sitting there.

"Mom?" He questioned. She wasn't looking at him. In fact, she hadn't really looked up since he pulled into the driveway.

"Mom, what are you doing here?" he asked, amazed to see her.

He couldn't think of a single reason for her to be on his porch. Not after how she and his father had treated him.

Hell, he'd been back in Reidsville for a year and a half, and she hadn't bothered to speak to him – not when he called and left a message telling them he'd moved back and not when he was promoted to detective, which was a big story in *The Reidsville Rag*: "Local Promoted to Detective, Citizens Concerned About Qualifications." It was a half-page of homophobic rants from a few citizens questioning whether a fairy could protect them from crime. They pulled the story halfway through the morning when he called and cursed out Mr. Flague, threatening to make his life a living hell, but the damage had been done.

Mrs. Gentry was a small-framed woman, about five feet and 4 inches tall. Her hair was gray now – it had been dark brown last time Isaiah had seen her – and was wrapped up in a tight bun on top of her head. After a few false starts, she finally spoke:

"I… I heard you got shot," she said softly.

"Yep," Isaiah replied.

"I didn't know. Not until tonight. I ran into Freda at the grocery store, and she said… said… you'd been shot and had been in the hospital. And I didn't know."

"Mom, I don't mean to be an asshole, but what are you doing here?"

"What do you mean? You're my son and I heard you got shot. I'm here to check on you."

"It's a little late to play the loving mother, isn't it?"

Gentry shot at her. "Mom, I'm sorry, but I really need to get inside and get to bed. I'm exhausted. Thanks for stopping by."

"Isaiah, I…." she started.

Now standing she looked a little more like the mother he remembered. Short, small, and unimposing. But her impact on him had been vast, causing her to take up much more space in his world than her small body did. Tears welled in her eyes.

"I just wanted to make sure you were okay."

With that, she walked down the stairs onto the walkway and cut through the grass to her car on the street. Isaiah hadn't noticed it there in the darkness. He was left confused and triggered. He'd done a lot of work in therapy to heal from the wounds his parents had inflicted on him. It had been traumatizing to learn he had nothing in common with them. The only thing they shared were the memories of their treatment of him, and that wasn't good enough for him to be interested in rebuilding a relationship with them. Seeing her, though, reminded him how much it hurt not to have a family. He looked back and saw his mother in the passenger seat of the vehicle – his father in the driver's seat looking straight forward. Without ever looking at Isaiah his father sped off into the Carolina summer night.

Isaiah slept like a baby that night and arose feeling refreshed. He was surprised, given what he had endured the past several days, following an unwelcome visit from his parents whom he hadn't seen in years. He knew his body must have been in desperate need of rest if he slept that well after the day he'd had - he'd even slept in and would be late for work. He texted Johnson and Tingles to say he would be late arriving, then took his time showering, dressing, and eating breakfast. The morning was unnaturally calm. Gentry didn't have many neighbors and none that were in view of his home, but he usually heard traffic in the mornings. All he heard that day were birds chirping and the occasional plane flying overhead. He enjoyed the peace. It's what he'd always loved about the country - the quiet and serenity. He'd almost moved to Charlotte, North Carolina to join their police force, but after visiting for the first time when he was 26, he decided it was too much for him. He needed to see the stars at night, unhindered by city lights, and he needed to hear the birds chirping in the mornings. Reidsville had a lot of hurtful memories attached to it, but it was home, and it gave him peace.

When he was sure he was ready to go, Gentry grabbed his keys, his Glock, and his phone and swung open his front door. Distracted, he made his way onto the porch, locked his door, and turned to head down his porch stairs.

Once he turned to face his yard, he dropped everything he was holding and froze, eyes fixed on the sight before him. His heartbeat skyrocketed and he felt himself begin to sweat. Standing erect in the middle of his yard was a tall stake, a circle of Evita flowers around the base, with a head on top. Gentry recognized the head - the black hair, the pale skin, bags under the eyes…..

Joseph DeCordts.

CHAPTER FIFTEEN

Within the hour the entire police force was at Gentry's home. Isaiah had instructed Johnson to send a few officers to Mrs. DeCordts' home and stay there. She wouldn't like it, but both of her sons had been murdered. If they weren't sure before, they surely knew now their suspect was targeting the DeCordts family. In the time between calling the force and them arriving, Gentry sat down on his porch and took note of anything he could from where he was. He didn't want to approach the stake and risk tampering with evidence. He knew he wouldn't be considered a suspect, but he didn't want to give anyone a chance to suspect him regardless. Once he'd discovered Joseph's head the chirping birds and overhead airplane sounds had ceased to exist. All he could focus on was Joseph's head; it appeared as if his dark eyes were staring directly at him. As he observed he couldn't help but think of who might be responsible. In a matter of twelve hours - less, even - their suspect, presumably a female, had murdered another man, decapitated him, drove a stake in Gentry's yard, and displayed the victim's head on it without being detected. Not only was their suspect agile, but strong. Joseph hadn't been a large man, and certainly not a muscular guy, but he was tall and likely weighed roughly 160-175 pounds. That much dead weight wouldn't be easy to move around single-handedly. So, either they had more than one suspect to find or theirs was a damn impressive villain in her own right.

Tingles and Johnson were the first to arrive. Gentry noted the two seemed to have gotten close, something he was curious about but in no state to discuss that morning. He filed the detail away for another time. The two fawned over him, ensuring he was okay and commenced questioning him on what he'd done the night before and that morning.

Had anything seemed out of place? *Only his parents.*

Had he heard anything? *No.*

Had he seen anything? *No.*

Had he noticed any cars following him from the station where he dropped them off the night before to his home? *No.*

He was already exhausted by the questions. The medical examiner and forensic team had arrived during the questioning and began taking prints. The medical examiner determined by the condition of the head the time of death must be between 2 and 3am. Joseph had only been dead a matter of hours.

Why didn't he let us protect him? Gentry thought.

After they questioned him, Gentry went back to being their colleague. He told them he thought there could be two suspects based on the physical ability necessary to overtake, murder, and decapitate two grown men. The others agreed it was possible. Tingles pointed out there was a circle of <u>Evitas</u> around the stake and wondered where the murderer got them from. If Martha had been the only supplier for a hundred miles or so, then their killer had traveled a long way to acquire them. Unless the killer knew how to grow them. The woman who'd opened the safe deposit box - their murderer - had told the bank manager she was interested in gardening, furthering the assumption their murderer knew Martha.

Gentry asked if they'd made much progress looking through the old case notes from the Southern murder, and after an awkward moment of the two talking over each other, they agreed they had not, in fact, made much progress. Gentry brushed off the awkward moment as something he didn't want to know about and suggested they get to the station. The officers Johnson had sent to Mrs. DeCordts' home had notified her of the death of her son, and they decided to give her time to process it. After all, whether she was hiding anything or not she'd lost her entire family in a year. They would focus some time on getting through the rest of those case notes. Gentry was sure Tingles was right - there was something there that would help them.

Back at the station they settled into the conference room and split the paperwork three ways. They'd given Donna strict instructions they were not to be disturbed and gotten straight to work. For hours, the three of them sifted through paperwork, reading every line on every paper. They read through interview transcripts and notes officers had made. They reviewed lists of evidence which had been collected at the crime scene and tried to connect something to Brent or Mrs. DeCordts. Nothing. They couldn't find anything out of the ordinary. No stone had been unturned, no question unasked, and no alibi unchecked. They were at another standstill despite Joseph's confession that his brother and mother were not where they said they were the night of the murder. Tingles leaned back in his seat and rubbed his eyes underneath his glasses.

"Shit," he hissed.

"Yeah," Gentry said, his tone echoing Tingles' defeat.

"The two of y'all sound plum pitiful," Johnson remarked.

"What do you mean?" Tingles asked.

"So, we didn't find what we hoped for at first glance. We just give up?"

"Nobody's giving up," Tingles said. "But maybe the answer just isn't *here*," he said, gesturing to the papers scattered across the conference room table. "It's certainly frustrating, though. This case has haunted me for thirty-five years."

"So, let's think about what we know," Johnson said. His energy rubbed off on Gentry who sat upright in his chair, ready to walk through the details they knew again.

"Okay, Darren Southern's time of death was approximately 10pm the night of the murder," Gentry started. "His wife, Clara, was at a gala and had at least fifteen people verify she was there until late that evening, so her story of finding him dead tracks. We know, by all accounts, Darren had no enemies, *but* there was friction between him and Paul, and he was possibly having an affair with Mrs. DeCordts. We also know she and Brent were not home for several hours the night of the murder, and she forced her entire family to lie about it. Given what we do know, there's *no way* the DeCordts are not the key to this murder," Gentry finished.

"And whoever our suspect is for the murder of the DeCordts brothers knows something about the murder of Darren Southern," Tingles said casually. His energy hadn't matched Johnson and Gentry's yet. "Like I've said, perhaps our suspect knows that one of the DeCordts murdered Darren Southern and is seeking revenge," he said. "But who?"

"Didn't you say the Southerns had a daughter?" Johnson asked.

"One. Shelly. She was three years old when her father was murdered. Home at the time but found hiding in her bedroom closet. The officers did ask her a few questions, but no one was able to get her to talk. A psychologist determined she must have found her father dead and been traumatized by the sight. The gunshot would have scared her, too, young as she was Likely sent her running."

"Thought she wasn't questioned," Gentry said.

"She was never *officially* questioned given that she could barely speak," Tingles explained. "Might not have been the best course of action, but her mother did a good job of gatekeeping her."

"Where is she now? Maybe she remembers something and would talk to us."

"I'd made a note to find her. I'm not sure. Let's see if we can. I doubt she knows much, young as she was."

"I'll see what I can dig up on her," Gentry said, rising from the table.

"I'll check in on the officers looking after Mrs. DeCordts," Johnson offered.

"I think I'll join you, Johnson. We should really pay Mrs. DeCordts another visit. No more mister nice fairy," he finished, winking.

With that, the three of them went about their tasks. Gentry moved to his office and started searching for the Southern's daughter, Shelly. He located birth records - March 29th, 1986, was her date of birth. Clara and Darren Southern were listed as the parents. Shelly's had been a premature birth according to the hospital records he discovered. She was hospitalized for the first three months of her life. Visitation records showed her father, Darren, visiting every single day - some days from 8am to 8pm, the duration of visiting hours. Clara, on the other hand, only visited two or three times a week. Gentry found this odd. Usually, the mother would be the one visiting daily, staying all day, and the father would continue to work. *Why hadn't Clara taken more interest in her daughter?* Gentry wondered.

The more he discovered about the Southerns, the more he wanted to know. Particularly the lives of Clara and Shelly after Darren's death. It wasn't lost on Gentry that, again, he felt embarrassed for not thinking about the Southerns before that moment. If Sara, like his officers had said, went missing after Darren's death, why hadn't they considered her involvement in Brent's murder earlier? For them to be related to the richest family in the town - hell, the richest family in the county - there was little to no information about them following Darren's death. Gentry searched for *anything* - schools Shelly had attended, or jobs Clara had held, newspaper stories, school transcripts… but *nothing*. After Darren's death, Clara and Shelly Southern ceased to exist.

"What the fuck is it with people going missing in this town?" Gentry mumbled to himself.

He kept digging until he found a legal filing for a testamentary trust account in Shelly Southern's name. Gentry was only vaguely familiar with testamentary trusts and had to conduct an internet search to understand it.

"Testamentary trusts are created upon someone's death," he read aloud. "They are dictated by someone's last will and testament…"

Gentry went back to the trust document which, according to his internet search, had only been made public record during the probate proceedings following Darren's death. He hadn't seen many trust documents and wasn't sure if the one he was looking at was traditional or not. Further, he couldn't be sure it hadn't been redacted due to the nature of the document. The first page laid out the essential information:

GRANTOR/TRUSTOR/SETTLOR: Darren Southern, with a mailing address 4459 Richardson Dr., Reidsville, NC, 27320

TRUSTEE: Shelly Southern, with a mailing address 4459 Richardson Dr., Reidsville, NC, 27320

THE SCHEDULE OF TRUST PROPERTY attached

hereto and made part hereof shall be held in a <u>private trust</u> and administered and/or distributed as provided in this agreement.

Gentry read the articles following. In the event of his death, the trust was to be formed in Shelly's name and was to be paid out to her in monthly increments once she turned eighteen. The two provisions set forth in the articles were a) Shelly had to be enrolled in college to receive the trust payments, and b) Shelly would have to undergo a paternity test to qualify. Gentry wasn't sure he'd read it correctly. *A paternity test?* Why in hell would she need to take a paternity test? As he read further, the trust articles specified the following:

As is the tradition in the Southern family trusts, all trustees are required to undergo paternity testing to validate blood relations before any funds are granted...

Etcetera. So, everyone was required to do it if they were a trustee. Gentry leaned back in his chair wondering, "If Shelly had received this trust, why couldn't he find her?" He shifted again, leaning towards the computer again, and continued looking through any file he could locate. Shelly would have to be over eighteen years of age now, which meant a paternity test would have been conducted. He'd likely need a search warrant to obtain it….

"Unless…." he muttered, in complete shock at the document he'd loaded on his P.C. Shelly Southern's trust had been contested by Darren's parents. *"That's* why this is a public record," Gentry said to himself.

As he read, he discovered Darren's parents believed Shelly to be the offspring of another man (unnamed) and demanded a paternity test be conducted immediately. But where are the resul…

"Holy shit!" he exclaimed loudly. "Ho… ly. Shit!"

CHAPTER SIXTEEN

Gentry couldn't wait to get Tingles on the phone. He grabbed his keys and raced to his SUV, speeding out of the parking lot to Mrs. DeCordts' home. If what he'd just learned had the implications he thought it did, they were pretty damn close to solving their case. No, cases: *both of them*. Gentry's excitement about this break in the case outweighed the fear of finding a decapitated head on a stake in his front yard. In fact, he'd nearly forgotten about it in the excitement. Tingles would be thrilled; of that, he could be sure. He approached the DeCordts' home and saw Johnson's patrol vehicle parked in front. *Good*, he thought. He hadn't missed them. He got out, rushed up the walkway to the door, rang the bell, and waited impatiently for an answer. Finally, Kimmie swung the door open.

"You look like shit," she said abruptly, looking him

up and down.

"Yeah. You too," he replied. "I need to see Tingles immediately."

"He's in there," she said, gesturing towards the sitting room they'd been in several times.

Gentry walked into the sitting room where he silently gestured for Tingles to come out and speak with him. Tingles obliged, and Gentry whispered they needed to speak privately. He had sensitive information to share. The two made their way outside so he could deliver his news.

"What have you found out, hunny?" Tingles asked with a confused chuckle. "You've marched me out here on a walk that took forty days and forty nights in 90-degree weather, and…"

"Shelly Southern is not Darren's daughter," he blurted out, cutting Tingles off. "She's *Paul's* daughter."

His words lingered between them. Tingles' eyes had grown wide, and, despite the heat, this information gave him goosebumps. *This. This* was the piece of information he'd been waiting for. The information that would break the case.

"So, we have a girl who is the heiress of a fortune, found out not to be the biological child of a Southern, but who *is* the child of the man accused of murdering Darren. Mrs. DeCordts wasn't having an affair. Paul was. Did she know?"

"Of course she knew." Kimmie's voice pierced

through the August heat, startling the detectives who hadn't seen or heard her approach. "Think she's oblivious?"

"You knew Paul was having an affair?" Gentry asked.

"Yep. What I didn't know is Shelly was his daughter. Thank you," she added triumphantly. Gentry hated her smug expression.

"All the same," Tingles started, "I'd like to ask her myself."

"I…." Kimmie dragged out the word. "I don't think that's a good idea," she finished.

"And why not? Something to hide?" Tingles asked.

"She's just lost her second child in a week," Kimmie said. "Jackass."

"And if she wants the person responsible apprehended, she'll need to cooperate with us," Tingles shot back.

With those words, he rounded Kimmie and marched towards the house. Gentry followed, and Kimmie grunted in frustration, following behind him. In less than a minute Tingles stood in front of Mrs. DeCordts, speaking urgently:

"Mrs. DeCordts, please excuse my directness. I know you've been through quite an ordeal the past couple of weeks, but I have some urgent questions that I believe honest answers will help us find the person responsible for these crimes. Were you aware that your husband was having an affair with Clara Southern?"

The room fell silent. Mrs. DeCordts' gaze became distant, and her cheeks blood red. Tingles didn't know if she was angry, surprised, hurt, or all three.

"Yes. I knew," Mrs. DeCordts said, surprisingly confident despite her expression.

"Did you know Shelly was his child?" Tingles asked.

With this, Mrs. DeCordts stood, walked over to Tingles, her high heels slowly clacking against the hardwood floor, and looked him directly in the eyes.

"Get the fuck out of my house, you lying fairy!"

Tingles didn't move. He knew he'd surprised her which told him she wasn't responsible for Darren's death. If, for some reason, she'd have wanted to kill him as some sort of revenge against Clara she wouldn't be as surprised as she was right now.

"Why did you lie to us about where you and Brent were the night of Darren's murder?"

"Get. The. Fuck. OUT OF MY HOUSE!" Mrs. DeCordts screamed at Tingles.

Johnson had risen, ready to peel the woman away from Tingles, but she stepped back. After a moment, tears began streaming down her face and she dropped back into her chair, throwing her hands over her face. The room was silent again, save for Mrs. DeCordts sobbing.

"Mrs. DeCordts," Tingles said. "It is not my

intention to be cruel here. I know what I said hurt you. But we have at least three people dead – two of which, are your children – and our solving this case hinges on your honesty with us. Please. Why were you and Brent out of the house on the evening of Darren Southern's murder? Why did you lie to us?"

Mrs. DeCordts stopped sobbing and looked up at Tingles.

"I'm done talking to you," she said. "If you want anything from me in the future – go through my attorney. Now get out!"

Tingles, Gentry, and Johnson headed through the hallway and out the front door. With or without Mrs. DeCordts, Tingles was determined to solve these cases once and for all.

Back at the station Tingles, Gentry, and Johnson huddled again in the conference room. Again, they'd given Donna instructions not to disturb them unless the town was on fire or Mrs. DeCordts asked to see them - and they all knew that wouldn't happen. Tingles was the first to speak. He was energized by the new information he'd obtained and felt indebted to Gentry for uncovering it. It finally made sense, however, why he couldn't find the puzzle piece - it would never have occurred to him to dig into the Southern's daughter.

"Gentleman, thanks to Detective Gentry we have some very valuable information. That Shelly Southern is the daughter of Paul DeCordts and Clara Southern tells us we've been looking at the Southern murder all wrong. We now know Cheryl and Darren were likely not engaged in an affair, but Paul and Clara certainly were. The question is who knew about the affair? Who knew Shelly was the daughter of Paul and Clara?"

"Well, Darren's family contested the testamentary trust intended for Shelly because they had doubts about her relation to the Southerns," Gentry offered. "If they suspected something, it's possible someone else did. Should we see if there's a family member we can question? I'm still looking for Shelly. There's absolutely *no* record of her after her father's death. I mean *nothing*."

"She changed her name," Tingles said, confidently. "It's the only thing that makes sense. Darren's family contests the trust. A paternity test is conducted to test her relation to them, and they discover she's not a blood relative, effectively disqualifying her *and* her mother from any of the Southern money. So, what would they do if they were interested in starting over and washing off the shame of a controversy? They'd change their names and move away. We need to see if we can find name change records for them. Can we do it now?"

"Let me grab my laptop," Johnson volunteered.

He left the room and returned in less than a minute. Gentry rounded the table and sat next to him - Johnson had good intentions, but he was slow as molasses on a computer, and Gentry didn't have the patience for it. He slid the laptop over in front of him with no protest from Johnson and began typing away. A few minutes later, with Tingles and Johnson watching with bated breath, Gentry stopped with a "*Shit!*"

"What have you found?" Tingles interjected before Gentry had a chance to continue.

"Goddamn record is sealed," Gentry said. There's a court document here for Clara and Shelly but… it's fuckin' sealed."

"I can call Judge Patterson and see if we can get them unsealed," Johnson said, getting up from the table.

"If we can get those records unsealed," Tingles started, "then I guarantee you we'll find the names we *should* be looking for. In the meantime, let's go talk to a Southern."

CHAPTER SEVENTEEN

Locating a Southern proved much easier than locating Clara and Shelly. Since they were the richest family in the town, they were also the most popular. Everyone either knew a Southern or knew who they were. Darren's mother, Agatha Southern, was still living and in excellent health. At eighty-nine years old, she still oversaw the operations of the Southern Bank, and although her other son James (everyone called him Jimmy) and *his* son Bruce ran the bank, every major decision still went through her. Gentry had reached out to her to ask if he and Tingles might schedule a meeting with her. They were happy to visit her at her home if it would be easier, he'd said. She'd responded that just because she was old didn't mean she was an invalid, and she would come to the station and speak with them there. She was happy to do whatever she could if it meant her son's murder would finally be solved. Gentry and Tingles set about getting a list of important questions together but ultimately decided they'd play it by ear. The few things they really needed to know were whether she knew where Clara and Shelly had gone, who knew about Paul and Clara, and if there was anything else she thought they needed to know.

Gentry slept at the Reidsville Inn that evening. His yard was still a crime scene, and if he was being honest, he didn't want to look at the spot where he'd seen a head displayed. In the past few weeks, he'd seen things he never anticipated. Two decapitated heads were something out of horror movies. Something the police academy hadn't done well was prepare him for *that*, and he was stuck with the knowledge he'd never forget those sights. He was now one of those cops who would grow old and tell young people, "I've seen things. I've seen things, man." So, he slept at the Reidsville Inn where there was always a room for rent. Tingles offered to ride with him to his home long enough to grab clothes and necessities for a few days, then back to the inn where he landed a room right next to Tingles. The two of them grabbed Chinese takeaway on the way to the inn and ate in Gentry's room while Tingles forced him to watch Judy Garland in *A Star is Born*. They turned in early, each hoping to get a good night's sleep before questioning Agatha Southern.

Neither of them got the good night's sleep they'd hoped for, but it was adequate. Gentry text Tingles to meet him at the car at 7:00am sharp so they'd have time to stop for coffee and breakfast on the way in. By 7:30am they arrived at the station, and Agatha Southern was due to arrive at 8:00am. As Gentry walked by Donna, he began to request they not be disturbed.

"I know, I know… don't bug ya'," Donna had said, cutting him off.

"You know me well," he said as he passed through the doors to the station.

Twenty minutes later Donna's voice came over the office intercom in Gentry's office. "Sir, Agatha Southern is here…. With her lawyer."

"Son-of-a-bitch," Gentry muttered after telling Donna to show them in. "I hadn't counted on that."

"Oh, I did," Tingles said, chuckling slightly. "It won't be a problem. She wants her son's case solved, and she'll do what it takes to make sure that happens. I'm sure of it."

"Hope you're right," Gentry said as he heard a light knock on the door and looked up to see Donna gesturing Agatha and her lawyer in.

Agatha was an average woman - approximately five feet and six inches tall and thin. Her hair was snow white and full, pulled back into a ponytail that cascaded halfway down her back. For an eighty-nine-year-old woman, her skin was surprisingly tight around her muscles; Tingles noted she looked *fabulous* and didn't appear to have had any cosmetic surgery done. The lawyer was the opposite of Mrs. Southern. He was tall, standing about six feet and four inches tall, and no less than two hundred and fifty pounds. He appeared middle-aged, reasonably attractive, Tingles noted, with dark hair and eyes. He looked mean, though. The four of them exchanged pleasantries, and Gentry invited everyone to sit down. They'd arranged two chairs for Gentry and Tingles on one side of the desk and the chairs for Agatha and her lawyer on the other. Once everyone was seated, the attorney spoke first. He asked if Gentry and Tingles minded if he recorded the interview. They said they didn't if he didn't mind them recording. Everyone agreed the interview would be recorded, and once it had commenced, the attorney continued.

"My name is Thomas Brine, I'm Agatha's attorney. I'm only here as a precaution. Agatha has informed me she is willing to cooperate with you and answer any questions you may have regarding her son and his murder. I don't plan to do much talking."

"Mrs. Southern," Gentry started.

"Agatha. Please," she replied calmly, kindly. Gentry was surprised by her soothing demeanor given everything he knew about her shrewd business sense and authoritarian approach to being the matriarch of her family.

"Agatha," Gentry said, smiling at her. "Thank you for agreeing to meet with us. As I'm sure you've heard we recently found a head in a safe deposit box in your bank. The investigation of that murder has led us back to investigating the murder of your son. We believe they are related." Gentry paused here, giving Agatha an opportunity to interject but she didn't. Tingles picked up the conversation.

"Agatha, it's nice to see you again," Tingles said. "As you know, I was the lead detective on your son's case thirty-five years ago. I'll get right to the point. We have discovered Shelly Southern was not actually your granddaughter. Can you tell us about how you found out?"

"Certainly," Agatha began, visibly surprised by the question.

She spoke clearly, loudly, and with precision, however. If anyone suspected Agatha Southern was "just some old woman," they had another coming from this eighty-nine-year-old matriarch.

"I always thought that girl looked like Paul DeCordts. The man had severe features. He was attractive enough, sure, but he had distinctive features and so did Shelly. Her jawline was like his; her nose was his; even her ears were shaped like his. I knew from the moment she was born she was not Darren's child. I tried to tell him, but he wouldn't listen. Our only saving grace was the clause written into the trust documents that would require the girl to have a paternity test before any trust funds would be released to her. That article has been written into every trust for every

Southern child since the first trust my great-grandfather opened for his children. He didn't trust his wife - she was a harlot before they married and you know what they say - you can take the whore out of the trailer park, but not the trailer park out of the whore…"

She paused with this and asked for a glass of water. Gentry excused himself and returned with the requested water. After a couple of sips Agatha continued:

"When Darren was murdered Shelly was three years old. She wasn't eligible for the trust until she was eighteen, but I didn't see any reason to prolong the anticipation of a trust I knew she'd never get. So, I contested the trust on the grounds that she was not the biological daughter of my son, and it would be cruel to allow her and her mother to wait fifteen years to find out. A judge agreed, ordered the test, and lo and behold - I was right."

"How did Clara and Shelly react to your contesting the trust?" Gentry asked.

"Clara was furious, but of course she knew Shelly wasn't Darren's. Clara came from a poor family here in town - all dead now, I'm afraid. I told Darren when he started dating that girl it wasn't worth it. Her father was a drunk and her mother rumored to be a whore. Only trouble would come from dating so *far* outside his class - stick to your own people. He wouldn't listen. He *loved* her, he said. I never trusted her. When I contested the trust, she lost her mind.

Showed up at my home screaming at my late husband and me. How dare we insinuate Shelly wasn't Darren's - as if we wouldn't find out later. I told her she had nothing to worry about if Shelly was Darren's child. She didn't want to hear it."

Agatha's matter-of-fact tone landed on Tingles and Gentry as callous. She didn't seem to care for poor people, her son's feelings, or those of a three-year-old child. Money was the important factor for her, and she wasn't going to give any to anyone who didn't deserve it by virtue of their relation to her. She could hardly be blamed – life had hardened an otherwise kind, intelligent, and beautiful woman. The pressure of holding her family's business together had resulted in her becoming direct, business-minded, and, at times, callous. She'd learned how to "play with the big boys."

"Once the results came in," she continued, "She went into hiding. Fine by us - at that point, she wasn't any relation to us, and neither was the child. None of us had any business with each other."

"Do you have any idea where they went?" Tingles asked.

"No. They were out of our lives, and we wanted it that way. I suspect Clara was too embarrassed to face us."

"And you never saw Shelly again?"

"I thought I did years later. Here in town," Agatha answered, airily as if she were recalling a fond memory. An abrupt change of tone. "I was walking down the street downtown and would swear I saw her on the other side of the road, but… cars were passing by, and I couldn't get a good look at her. Besides, it had been nearly twenty years since I'd seen her as a three-year-old. By the time traffic cleared she was gone, so who knows."

"What can you tell us about Darren?' Gentry asked. "Maybe understanding who he was will help us understand his case."

"Darren was smart but too nice," Agatha started. "Always kept him in some kind of trouble - Clara, for example. He couldn't see the world for what it was. He trusted everyone. I kept telling him people would take advantage of the rich at every opportunity. There was a little boy in his grade school class he befriended - Timmy. Timmy's family lived in a trailer park. His father was a cashier at Chilton's Gas Station, and his mother collected a disability check. Darren brought him over to our home every day after school for weeks. Suddenly I realized food was going missing from our refrigerator. I asked Darren if his friend was taking food from us, and he said it wasn't possible. The next day I caught Timmy red-handed, and he never came back. There is a slew of similar stories. Paul DeCordts wasn't a wealthy man. Darren fronted most of the money to establish that law firm and put in most of the work. Paul DeCordts took advantage of him."

"Interesting," Mr. Tingles said out loud. He was lost in thought now. Gentry thought he witnessed the moment Tingles disconnected from the interview and entered his own world. Something had clicked and he was eager to find out what it was.

"Mrs. Southern…" Gentry started and then, seeing Agatha's expression of protest, "Agatha. What do you know about The DeCordts' children? Brent and Joseph?"

"Not much," Agatha said. "I didn't spend a lot of time around them, but I remember Brent had a temper. There was an afternoon when Paul and Darren planned a cookout at Darren's home to celebrate a big court win - thanks to Darren, of course. Brent had begged his mother for another piece of cake, and she'd told him no over and over. He became enraged. So much so he picked up that whole cake and threw it across the yard. It didn't take much to make him angry."

"What about Joseph?" Gentry asked.

"He was a calm boy. Too quiet for comfort. You know too loud or too quiet is always a red flag when it comes to people. But he was sweet."

By now, they'd been in Gentry's office for nearly an hour. Tingles had snapped back to reality and aimed for the last question.

"Agatha, can you tell us anything else about your son, Clara, Shelly, or the DeCordts you think we should know?

Anything that might help us solve these murders?"

"I don't know if I have anything useful, detective. What I can tell you, in retrospect, is the rumors of Cheryl and Darren having an affair eclipsed what was really going on between Darren's and Paul's families. That's why you couldn't find his killer, Mr. Tingles."

"Do you believe your son's murder was related to Clara's infidelity?" Tingles asked.

"No. I believe *his* murder was related to the rumor that he was sleeping with Cheryl. I believe the reason you never found his killer is because you believed that rumor."

Agatha's pointed words lingered for several moments before she said,

"Is there anything else I can do for you, detectives?"

"No," Gentry said. "You've been very helpful, Agatha. We really appreciate your time. Would it be okay to call if we have additional questions?"

"Certainly."

"I have one or two more questions," Tingles interjected as everyone was standing.

"I'm all ears," Agatha said.

"When you discovered Shelly was not your granddaughter, validating the fact Paul and Clara had had an affair, why didn't you tell the police? Especially if you believed the false rumor about Darren was the key to solving your son's murder."

"Our family had been through an ordeal, Mr. Tingles," Agatha said. This was the first time she'd shown emotion, and it wasn't subtle. Almost immediately tears began welling in her eyes. "My son was dead, and although I knew she wasn't related, I still felt like I was losing my only grandchild. Though, I could have cared less about Clara."

And she's back, Tingles thought.

"Did Paul know Shelly was his?"

"I don't know," Agatha said. "But as angry as she was over my contesting the trust and demanding a paternity test before she turned eighteen, I'd say so."

"Thank you, Agatha," Mr. Tingles said.

Everyone bade their farewells, and Agatha left with her attorney. Tingles and Gentry sat in silence for several minutes until Tingles spoke.

"We need to find out if Paul knew he was Shelly's father. If there's a record of a paternity test showing he's the father, that means a blood sample came from somewhere. Either he knew or that sample was obtained by someone, somehow. When was the test conducted?"

Gentry's cheeks turned red from embarrassment. He hadn't even checked. All he knew was he saw Paul DeCordts was Shelly's father and ran out the door to find Tingles with the development. He turned to his laptop and navigated to the documents he'd found. Tingles leaned in once the test results had been loaded onto the screen.

"February 5th, 2022," Tingles read. "This document has her name on it. The only document we've found that has Shelly Southern's name on it."

"That doesn't make sense. She was thirty-six years old when this test was conducted," Gentry said. "You mean to tell me there's no record whatsoever of her between 1989 and 2022? And if this test was conducted in 2022, how could Agatha have been so certain of the results back then?"

"Because the test conducted on Shelly was only intended to tell them if Darren was her father. They didn't care who the real father was. Let's see if Johnson was able to get those records unsealed," Tingles said. "I have a feeling that will answer a lot of questions."

CHAPTER EIGHTEEN

Johnson had reached Judge Patterson's secretary who informed him the judge was inaccessible until the following morning. They'd have to wait on getting the records unsealed, putting them at somewhat of a standstill - at least that's what they decided in the interest of creating an evening off for themselves. In the past week they hadn't slept much except for Tingles' and Gentry's hospital stays. None of them could remember the last time they'd eaten a decent meal, either, so they decided to go to *Maeves*, a small Irish pub in downtown Reidsville. It was the only restaurant in town one could consider "nice," and only in the way one considered changing clothes if they had on jeans and a t-shirt, but nonetheless didn't guarantee one *would*, in fact, change clothes. It was a Saturday evening, and the place was packed with people. The sounds of conversation rushed footsteps from one end of the restaurant to the other by wait staff, and the clinking of silverware on the dish echoed in every corner of the room. The three took their places at the bar - no tables were available and the hostess all but laughed at them for asking. Each ordered a cocktail and waited patiently for it while looking at the menu. Johnson frequented the place, so he didn't need to look but he did anyway.

"Maybe tonight I'll be adventurous and try something new," he said. He wouldn't.

Tingles looked around the establishment taking it all in. Reidsville had surely progressed in the years since he'd been back. He wondered if Eden had and chuckled to himself at the absurdity of that thought. As he scanned the room, he noticed none other than Kimmie Flague seated at a table in the far corner. She sat across from two people with their backs to him, but he could tell neither of them was Cheryl DeCordts. Tingles turned his gaze away from her hoping she wouldn't notice, but he discreetly pointed her out to Johnson and Gentry. Gentry's eyes found her in the crowded room and tried to look without drawing her attention. In a fleeting moment, when the crowd had cleared enough, Gentry recognized the two people sitting across the table from Kimmie - his parents.

"*Shit,*" he said slowly.

Johnson and Tingles looked over at him. By now he wasn't able to pull his gaze away. This was the second time he'd seen his parents in a week, more times than the past ten years combined, despite having lived in the same town for at least half of those.

"Everything alright?" Johnson asked.

"Um… yeah. I mean, my parents are here with Kimmie," Gentry answered. "Would it be okay if we found somewhere else to eat?"

"Of course," Tingles said, sympathetically.

Johnson agreed. Tingles recalled, Johnson telling him he had known the Gentrys most of his life. He grew up with Jackson Gentry, Isaiah's father, and hung out in the same circles as Susan, Isaiah's mother. Most people were surprised when the news about Isaiah being gay trickled through the rumor mills of Reidsville's gossip network, and Johnson was defending Isaiah. Most people proclaimed they would have reacted the same way if their son was a fairy. Johnson said to every one of them, "It's still their child, and they could have handled it better."

One autumn morning during that time, Johnson ran into Jackson Gentry at Chilton's Gas Station. Jackson was furious with him after hearing Johnson didn't think they'd handled their son's coming out well. They exchanged words, after which they never spoke again.

Mr. Tingles told Johnson and Gentry to go ahead, and he'd meet them outside. He waved down the bartender working on their cocktails from across the bar and noticed her calling to the kitchen for backup. A young blonde woman ran over to the bar where Tingles sat.

"We're going to have to leave. I'll pay the check, but we won't have time to drink them."

"No problem, suga. Don't I recognize you?" the woman asked.

Tingles looked at her for a moment and realized it was the young woman from Gigi's Floral Fabulosity.

"Ah, yes," Tingles said. "Christina. It's nice to see you again."

"You're that detective! I knew I recognized you. Good to see you, too, doll. I'll get your check."

As Tingles paid the check, tipped Christina, and got up from his barstool, he realized Johnson and Gentry hadn't made it out of Kimmie's sight in time. She'd spotted them which meant Gentry's parents knew they were there. Isaiah noticed Kimmie looking at him and saw his mother whip around, a look of longing on her face - she wanted to speak to her son; his father hadn't turned around at all.

Before Kimmie or his mother could get up to head their way, Isaiah was headed out the door, leaving Tingles and Johnson in his wake. He didn't want to ruin his only night off all week with more bullshit. In just a few short weeks, he'd seen two decapitated heads, been shot, seen Kimmie Flague enough to last a lifetime, and been ambushed by his mother whom he hadn't seen in a decade: he just wanted a reprieve from the surprises.

As he walked aimlessly down the street from *Maeves* he wondered if he'd made the right decision coming back to Reidsville. He hadn't thought about having to face the demons of his upbringing when he made the decision. All he'd considered was how he had the chance to prove everyone wrong about him. He'd show them he wasn't just some run-of-the-mill fag - he was different. Although, he didn't even know what a "run-of-the-mill" fag was. He'd still only ever met a handful of other queer people and, apart from the little he'd seen in the one queer nightclub he'd been to, didn't know anything about the culture he was supposed to be a part of. Here he was now, though, the queer police detective in his small, southern hometown and running away from the same things he'd spent his entire life running from. He stopped, turned around, and looked back towards *Maeves*.

"Fuck this," he said out loud and started walking back towards the restaurant. As he approached the building, he saw his mother emerge from the crowded entryway and stop as she saw him coming. He stopped, too, and they stood looking at each other for several moments. Susan took several steps forward, never taking her eyes off Isaiah. He couldn't read her expression. In the decade since he'd last seen her, she'd changed - her demeanor was different, her skin looser, her hair grayer, her eyes… more vacant. She thought he looked the same as he did when he left home. The thought made her stomach sink. He'd left home and never returned.

"Isaiah," she said softly. Her tone was almost begging. He didn't respond. "Isaiah, I've missed you," she said.

Still, he didn't respond.

"Isaiah, I know you're angry with your father and me. You have a right to be. We don't understand… you. But you're our son, and we love you, and…"

"You love me?" he shot at her. "You *love* me?" Rolling his eyes, he put his hands on his hips and started pacing. "That's rich, mom. For ten years you've ignored my existence. For ten years you've avoided my phone calls, never returned a Christmas or birthday card, hell, didn't even bother to call and congratulate me on making detective. But you love me, huh?"

"Isaiah, I can't take back…"

"No, you can't, mom. You can't take back ostracizing your only son. And you can't just pop back up because I got shot to tell me how much you love me, how sorry you are, and whatever else you came out here to say."

"Well, I am sorry, Isaiah." Her tone had become defensive. "I live with my decisions every day. For ten years, I've had to consider whether I made the right choice, and believe it or not, I know I didn't. I know I failed you."

"Knowing you failed me nor apologizing for it makes it any better," Isaiah said.

He'd stopped pacing and was looking into her eyes. He continued calmly:

"Mom, you and Dad hurt me. The two of you were the only family I had, and you abandoned me in favor of your religion. Then, after mentally, emotionally, and physically abusing me until I turned eighteen and got the fuck out of there, you acted like your only child was dead for over ten years."

"Physically?" Susan asked, tears welling in her eyes. "What do you mean physically?"

Isaiah could tell she was surprised - she didn't know. She had no idea his father had beaten the shit out of him relentlessly several times. He always hit below the neck so the bruises wouldn't show, and Isaiah wore pants and long sleeves no matter what the weather was like so he could hide them.

"Ask your husband," Isaiah said.

Eyeing Johnson and Tingles at the door, he swiftly moved past his mother and headed towards the car. Johnson followed closely behind him, but Tingles said he needed to use the restroom before they left and lingered at the door. When Isaiah and Johnson were out of view, he approached Susan who was standing in the same spot Isaiah had left her.

"Ma'am, I'm your son's friend and colleague, Mr.

Tingles," he began. Susan didn't respond, but Tingles had overheard the conversation and thought she was likely trying to process the news of finding out her husband had abused their child. "Respectfully, I think it'd be better if you leave Isaiah alone. If or when he's ready to speak to you he will certainly let you know."

"I just want…" she started to say through tears. "I wish none of this had ever happened. I wish we could be happy… be a family again."

"Which part do you wish were different?" Tingles asked. "The part where your son is estranged? Or the part where he's gay?"

Susan froze.

"Ma'am, he won't ever not be gay. But he will always be your son. Problem is, you can't see him for who he is because you're so fixated on that one thing that some old dusty book told you is unacceptable. When does love speak louder than hate? Sometimes showing up for the people we love, standing up for them, supporting them, and loving them is a choice we have to make when we don't understand who they are. You made the wrong choice and now you have to live with that. Have a good night."

Tingles turned and walked away from Susan. His last words floated in the air around her, and as he moved farther away from her, he felt like he'd said what he wanted to say to his own mother for decades.

CHAPTER NINETEEN

The following morning Johnson received a call from Judge Patterson. Johnson, together with Tingles and Gentry on speaker phone, presented their case for having Shelly Southern's sealed records unsealed. Judge Patterson was hesitant, but after some questioning and the trio's satisfactory answers, he relented and agreed. Since it was a Saturday the three of them would have to wait until Monday. The rest of the weekend was one of the longest Gentry could remember. All he wanted was to get his eyes on those sealed records and solve these cases. They were so close he could taste it. He didn't know how, but he had a feeling Shelly was the key to their case, they just needed to know *who* to look for.

Tingles agreed Shelly was the key to their case. She'd disappeared, along with her mother, which was already a red flag. Perhaps Clara *was* involved, Tingles had suggested. She could have put a hit on him, banking on the idea she would be entitled to his money as his wife, and then the plan backfired. She probably also believed her daughter would be able to avoid a paternity test and inherit the trust her father had left her, another backfired plan. This didn't explain the deaths of Brent and Joseph DeCordts, of course, but Tingles had never been surer of anything than he was at the fact that finding Shelly Southern was the missing piece to both puzzles.

The weekend came and went in a slow crawl, and on Monday morning Johnson, Tingles, and Gentry arrived at the station ready for action. Judge Patterson's order to unseal the files had been issued with urgency - Johnson had stressed they needed to find their killer and bring them to justice as soon as possible because the public was in danger. The order hadn't been processed yet, but they'd been assured they would have access Monday morning. In the meantime, they reviewed reports from the previous days' events. No fingerprints were found on Joseph's head, the stake on which it was displayed, or the Evita flowers on the ground around it. None of them were surprised. Fingerprints hadn't been found at any of the scenes - none in the bank, in Brent's home, or on Joseph. Forensics wouldn't solve this case for them - not this time.

While they discussed their next steps Officer Carter entered with a large box. He'd been demoted temporarily while his relationship with Kimmie was being investigated. He spent his days cleaning and doing receptionist duties until it was determined whether he would be allowed to remain on the force. Johnson looked up as Carter barged in - he was a muscular, albeit large man, so nothing he did was subtle. As he plopped the box on the table, he looked triumphant. Tingles and Gentry remained talking, not realizing Carter had entered and *stayed*. Carter cleared his throat to get their attention.

"I found a box of crime scene photos from the Southern case down in the archives," he said. "They were filed under D for Darren instead of S for Southern like the other box."

Carter looked proud, and his tone pleaded, "Please let this be good enough to keep me on the force."

"I'll be damned!" Tingles exclaimed, shooting up from his chair and hurrying over to the box. "I'd forgotten about all these photos - I can't believe I didn't ask."

"Is there anything good in there?" Gentry asked.

"I'm not sure," Tingles said, caressing the lid, but hesitating to open it.

"Well, let's open it," Johnson encouraged him. "See what's in there."

"I will, I will," Tingles said softly. "Somehow this feels different from those documents," he said, nodding at the files still strewn across the conference room table. "Photos make it real again."

"Can it get any realer than two decapitated heads?" Carter said, insensitively.

"What are you still doing here?" Johnson snapped. "Thanks for the box, now get out."

Carter grunted, frustrated, but did as he was told. Once the door snapped shut again, Tingles lifted the box open and stared down into the sea of disorganized Polaroids. The box was chock-full of photos. They'd have to divvy them up like the files and meticulously review them, looking for any clues they could possibly find. It would take days, maybe weeks. Right on top was a photo of Darren's corpse on the floor of his home. Tingles picked it up and was transported back to 1989. He'd been a detective in Greensboro at the time and was called in to assist with a homicide due to the victim's high-class status. The Reidsville Police Department and the mayor of the town wanted a quick investigation and resolution. They got neither, and Tingles got his first belt notch for an unsolved case.

As Tingles observed the photo, he could smell the room he'd stood in thirty-five years ago. The smell of death, paint (the Southerns had just had their dining room painted three days before the murder), and flowers. He remembered the stillness of the house. Despite the police officers moving around, the forensic team dusting for fingerprints, and Clara sobbing in the kitchen, he'd felt unnaturally calm. Even now the calmness made him uneasy. It was almost as if he'd been in the presence of evil in that house, and nearly forty years later he'd been handed the opportunity to hunt down and confront it. He continued to stare at the small Polaroid until something stood out to him - a small red flower lying on the floor above Darren Southern's head. Tingles could nearly draw a straight line from the bullet in his head to that flower. The Polaroid cut off the flower, but Tingles was sure of one thing -

"I'll be goddamned!" he exclaimed.

"What?" Johnson and Gentry said at once.

"Evita," he replied, almost in a trance. "There was an Evita flower at the Southern crime scene."

He'd tossed the photo on the table between Johnson and Gentry who leaned over the table to get a closer look. Tingles was maniacally digging through the box to find any photo of Darren's corpse he could find - he wanted a closer look at the flower, and there had to be a better photo of it. It took him a mere five minutes to rummage through the entire box, separating photos of Darren from the rest. Then he sifted through each one in silence as he looked for a more detailed photo of the flower, finally finding an angle that showed it in all its glory. He stared for several moments before another image stood out in the new photo.

"We need to find Shelly," he said, more to himself than anyone in the room.

Gentry and Johnson watched as Tingles laid out a handful of photos, all of Darren Southern's corpse.

"I was wrong," he said, as he finished organizing the photos in an order that made sense to him. "These photos are the key to this case I've been looking for, but I'd never realized it thirty-five years ago."

He stood back and looked at the photos laid out. The others could see his eyes move from one photo to the next and listened as he "Mhm'd" to himself.

"Tingles, you want to clue us in here?" Gentry asked.

"Come," Tingles said, motioning for Gentry to stand and look at the photos.[22] Johnson did the same, and Tingles was sandwiched between them, all three staring at the collage of crime scene photos.

"What do you see?"

"Is now really the time for a training session?" Gentry asked.

"Just... *look*," Tingles implored him.

After several minutes Gentry was about to give up when he saw it.

"Holy shit," he said.

"What the fuck am I missing?" Johnson interjected.

"Look very closely," Tingles said. "See that Evita flower?" He pointed it out.

"Yeah, I see the flo..." he started, and then, "Oh shit."

In a single photo, Tingles had spotted the corner of Shelly Southern's face, her father's body, an Evita flower, and a small handprint in Darren Southern's blood.

"Shelly saw the killer and probably knew them. Her little handprint is right next to her daddy's body in his blood. I can't believe we missed it. *How* did we miss it?"

"Doesn't matter now," Gentry said. "What matters is we see it now, and we know we need to find Shelly. If she can tell us who murdered her father, then that will lead us to our current murderer."

"Detective…" Tingles said. "We already know who our current murderer is."

Gentry and Johnson looked at Tingles like he'd gone mad. They exchanged glances, then looked back at him expecting him to continue but he didn't. Tingles was waiting for them to put the pieces together. When he realized they weren't even trying he broke the silence.

"Gentlemen, our killer is, without a doubt, Shelly Southern. She is the woman we are searching for."

"I don't follow," Gentry said. "How did you come up with that?"

"Yeah, you're gonna' have to help us out here, Tingles," Johnson said.

"Boysssss…" Tingles said in his queer southern drawl. "It's really quite obvious, isn't it? A three-year-old Shelly Southern saw her father, Darren, murdered in cold blood.

Then the only family she knew ostracized her because, unbeknownst to her at that age, she wasn't actually Darren's daughter at all, but Paul's. Of course, Paul also didn't want anything to do with the child, so she was effectively fatherless. That takes a toll on a young woman. So, she grew up bitter and angry at both families, but the DeCordts in particular seeing as a member of their family murdered Darren, the only father she would have had growing up. That Evita flower signals that a DeCordts is guilty. Detective Gentry, you may remember when we first visited Mrs. DeCordts she wore an Evita flower in her hair – along with Joseph's confession that irrefutably places her at the scene of Darren's murder. Shelly Southern is exacting her revenge."

"Do we really think Shelly is that elusive? I mean, she's carrying out a pretty elaborate plan to be hiding in the shadows somewhere," Gentry said.

"She's hiding in plain sight... I'd bet money on it," Tingles responded.

"Detectives!" A loud, excited voice pierced through the doorway as Donna burst into the room. "Detectives, Kimmie Flague called - Cheryl DeCordts has gone missing!"

CHAPTER TWENTY

etectives Gentry and Tingles made their way to meet Kimmie at the DeCordts home. They'd called and instructed her to stay put, not touch anything, and not speak to anyone except an attorney if she decided. For the past several days Kimmie had spent a lot of time with Cheryl DeCordts, so she was their best asset when it came to finding her. Besides, her entire family was dead. Tingles thought they must be getting too close for their killer's comfort - presumably Shelly Southern. In a matter of days, she'd murdered her second victim, and now the matriarch of the family had gone missing.

When they arrived at the DeCordts home Kimmie was sitting on the front porch smoking a cigarette. She looked disheveled, and that alarmed Tingles. Was she nervous because she was guilty of something or because she was afraid? As they approached the front door, which was standing wide open, Tingles concluded she must be afraid. The floor of the entryway of the home was strewn with Evita flowers and every piece of furniture from the door to the hallway was turned over. There had been a struggle. Tingles would expect nothing less from Mrs. DeCordts than to fight back. Tingles looked over at Kimmie just in time to see her light another cigarette with the butt of the one she'd just finished. She looked at him, wide-eyed, and he was certain in that moment she was genuinely terrified. He empathized, but he still didn't trust her.

Gentry stood next to Tingles looking inside. They decided they'd enter together once the other officers arrived. They'd need to examine the entire house. For now, however, Gentry wanted to question Kimmie. This would be a good opportunity to get some information out of her - anything she knew that they didn't. She was vulnerable and wanted to find Cheryl DeCordts.

"Kimmie, when's the last time you saw her?"

"This morning," Kimmie replied, her voice shaking. It was the first time either detective had heard her speak without a hint of condescension or sass.

"What time?" Gentry asked. His questions were short and direct. He was still thinking about her at the table with his parents at *Maeves*. He didn't want to speak to her at all, but duty called.

"Around seven. I had to leave and go to the office for

a while. Told her I'd be back in a couple of hours or so…"

Her voice trailed off as she finished the sentence, as if she might cry.

"Was there anything out of the ordinary this morning? With Mrs. DeCordts or in the neighborhood?"

"No. Nothing that I noticed," Kimmie replied, taking another drag of her cigarette and holding the smoke in her lungs long enough it hurt the detectives to look at her.

"Did Mrs. DeCordts have any home maintenance scheduled today? Lawn care, appliance maintenance, or anything of the kind?" Tingles asked.

"Not that I'm aware of," Kimmie said. "But she kept her calendar on the desk in the sitting room. If she did, it would be there."

"When did she find another supplier for the Evita flower?" Gentry asked, suddenly remembering the only local supplier of the flower had been shot and killed weeks earlier.

"I… I don't know," Kimmie said. "She hadn't mentioned anything to me other than she hated how she couldn't keep them in the house anymore."

"Kimmie, have you noticed anything the past few days? Anyone around in the neighborhood who doesn't belong? Maintenance workers who aren't usually around? Anything?"

"No, I… wait."

"What is it?" Tingles asked.

Kimmie looked over towards Brent DeCordts' house.

"The other night I stayed here with Cheryl. We'd been up late talking and drinking wine, and she didn't want me to drive so she made me stay here in one of the spare bedrooms. When I went upstairs, I thought I saw something moving in that window which you can see from here. Like a figure or something. But it was so fast - I kept looking and never saw anything else."

"Interesting," Mr. Tingles responded. "Our suspect must still be using the home to spy on this house. The question is - how is she getting inside?"

"She?" Kimmie asked. "You think whoever is doing this is a female?"

"We're almost certain," Gentry said.

Tingles was shocked by her surprise. If she didn't suspect the killer was a woman, that meant she didn't know anything worth knowing about their investigation. When she'd threatened to investigate on her own, he thought she might be more useful than she'd turned out to be. It appeared the only thing she'd known before them was where Joseph was, and that was only because she'd spent so much time with Cheryl. For a moment, Tingles felt sorry for her. She had the ambition of Barbara Walters, but nowhere near the talent. He remembered she had outed Gentry, however, and had managed to maintain a relationship with his parents which he'd longed for his entire life and stopped feeling sorry for her. She didn't deserve his or Gentry's empathy. Tingles noted Kimmie had picked up on the note of surprise in Gentry's response to her.

"You know, I didn't actually investigate," she said. "I just wanted to piss you off."

"Well, I guess that's why you didn't get in our way," Gentry responded. "Stay here for now. We're going to head inside."

By this time, the other officers had arrived. Tingles and Gentry led the way inside, warning the officers nothing should be touched or moved, which would be difficult given the flowers all over the floor. Tingles stressed to the officers how everything their suspect had done up to this point had a meaning. Their suspect was a fan of theatrics and Tingles wanted an opportunity to see their artwork from every angle possible. There could be a message in there somewhere that may lead them to the killer *and* Mrs. DeCordts. Tingles was convinced their suspect was Shelly Southern, but he was smart and experienced enough to know there was still a chance he could be wrong. If Shelly was their murderer, there would be more clues pointing to her at this crime scene, and since he knew no fingerprints had been left at any of the other crime scenes, they'd need to be more attentive and intuitive.

They had to tiptoe around the flowers so as not to disturb the way they were lying on the floor. They seemed to be just thrown but Tingles didn't want to risk it. Once he made it to the other side of the entryway he turned and looked at them again. As he stared into the flowers he was transported, again, back to 1989. It was as if he was looking at Darren Southern's body on the floor again and it hit him - the flowers were laid out like a body.

"Detective!" Tingles called loudly, followed by Gentry's approaching footsteps.

"What do we have?" Gentry asked.

"Look at how the flowers are laid out."

"Is that the shape of…"

"A body," Tingles finished Gentry's thought. "Do you remember the photo of Darren Southern's body? The Evita flower was above his head. These flowers are laid out like a body - meaning the head is pointing in the direction of Brent Southern's home."

"You think Shelly is trying to lure us there?" Gentry inquired.

"I'd bet my life on it," Tingles responded, a touch of pride in his voice that Gentry had followed along so quickly. "We can't just jump into it, though. We still can't be one-hundred percent certain Shelly is our suspect until we get…" Tingles' phone rang loudly, startling the detectives.

"*Shit!*" Tingles exclaimed. "That scared the gay right out of me." He answered as he chuckled at himself and listened intently to the voice on the other end.

"Mmhm… I see. Thank you." He disconnected the call and looked up at Gentry who waited impatiently.

"Well?" he asked.

"Shelly Southern's mother changed her name to Martha Raines," Tingles said. "And Shelly's to Christina Raines."

"Martha Raines? As in the woman who…"

"The very one," Tingles said, excitedly, cutting him off. "I would never have recognized her. She used to be so small," he added, pausing to think. "This explains Shelly's knowledge of gardening. If Martha was here all along, Shelly must be, too. We must find her."

Tingles tiptoed around the flowers and back out the door, confident they'd figured out what was meant for them inside the DeCordts' home.

"It makes sense Martha grew the Evita. Christina must have known her mother was the only supplier of the plant to Gigi's. And of course, she knew the flower had been left at the scene of Darren's murder, which is why it's her calling card now - assuming we're right and she's our murderer. Was there any evidence of anyone living with Martha when the home was searched?"

"No, it appeared she lived alone," Gentry said.

"I'll have Johnson dig around for Christina." Tingles added, pulling his phone back out. He walked out of earshot from Gentry who was left on the porch with an eavesdropping Kimmie.

"Sounds like you're making progress," she said.

"We just need to find Cheryl," Gentry responded.

"Do you think you know where she is?"

"Maybe," he replied. "I'm going to have an officer take you back to the station so you're safe. We'll take it from here."

Moments later, an officer escorted Kimmie to his car, and they pulled away, heading for the station. Tingles re-emerged from his phone conversation and immediately began positing his theory of events.

"Christina Raines, formerly Shelly Southern, witnessed the murder of the man she thought was her father. Her mother, knowing better about her biological father, did her best to protect Shelly, but she couldn't fight the Southerns' money and resources, so she was forced to admit Shelly was not Darren's child. Due to the affair the two of them were ostracized from the Southern family and left to survive on their own. To make life easier on them, Clara changed their names. It appears that at least Martha lived in seclusion - she likely did her shopping in surrounding towns to avoid the embarrassment she might have faced from people finding out what had happened. My guess is that Shelly - Christina - found out about her mother's past when she got older, and they became estranged. How else would she so callously murder her own flesh and blood? Not only that, but she remembered seeing who killed the man who had been her father, and I can guarantee you it was a DeCordts. It's the only thing that makes sense for her targeting them the way she has. I was wrong about one thing. The Evita at every scene was never meant for *us*; it was meant for *them*. To let them know she was coming for them."

"But why now?" Gentry asked. "And why every member of the family?"

"She's angry. Not only was her biological father not interested in her, but one of the DeCordts took away the only father she knew. She was young, but she knew she'd been abandoned."

"I don't know, Tingles. It's a little far-fetched, don't you think?"

"No. I know it is," he replied, with a confident smirk. "But I've no doubt I'm right. We just need to put the rest of the pieces together. *Shit!*"

Tingles' phone rang again, startling him as it had moments earlier and he promptly answered. Gentry heard what he thought was Johnson's voice on the other end but couldn't make out what he was saying. He waited patiently for a few minutes, listening to Tingles' end of the conversation, which consisted solely of "Mhms" and "I sees" again. Tingles hit the "end" button on his phone and turned to Gentry.

"Johnson pulled reports on Paul DeCordts' death a

year ago. His home-health nurse was reported missing just before his death. Around the same time, Mrs. DeCordts complained to the home-health company that they'd switched her nurse without notifying her."

"You think the new home-health nurse was Christina?"

"I'd stake my life on it. And if I'm right, *that's* how she got the blood sample for the paternity test, and she also murdered Paul DeCordts."

CHAPTER TWENTY-ONE

Mr. Tingles knew they'd have to exhume Paul DeCordts' body to prove his theory that Shelly Southern - Christina - had murdered Paul DeCordts (and likely the home-health nurse she replaced who was never found). It was the only thing that made sense to him. Why else would Mrs. DeCordts have been surprised by a new home-health nurse? Furthermore, it couldn't be a coincidence Paul had died the same day. He was a sick man, but according to the reports Johnson had obtained, he wasn't close enough to death then - not *that day* - to explain his sudden passing. The pieces were beginning to come together. Tingles was certain they'd identified their murderer and knew why she'd done it. What he hadn't figured out yet was who killed Darren Southern, but he was certain the answer would be revealed by the time their case was over.

After over three decades, Tingles was going to put the Darren Southern murder to rest.

Mr. Tingles and Detective Gentry made a call to Johnson to organize a raid on Brent DeCordts' home. If they were right that Christina was holding Cheryl hostage in the home, they needed to move as quickly as possible - they couldn't be sure how long she'd let Mrs. DeCordts live. Tingles thought to himself she must know they're on her heels. He thought she could be luring them into a trap and told Gentry as much. The two agreed they'd need to be careful, approaching everything they did with extreme caution, or otherwise, someone would end up dead. They devised a plan: Johnson would stay back at the station and call orders. He would brief the officers being sent to the home who would be instructed to arrive in unmarked cars without the use of their lights and sirens. They'd park away from the home, approach quietly on foot, and surround the home. They knew Christina was likely watching, so they had several officers stationed around the home at distances watching the home with telescopes. Two of the men were skilled "snipers" (otherwise known as hunters in the south): if Christina tried to shoot from a window, they'd see her first. Tingles and Gentry stayed stationed in Cheryl DeCordts' home. Each armed, they'd make their way up to Brent's home when it was time to raid.

Before any of their men were deployed to surround

the house on foot, they employed the skills of those watching from a distance - officers Brown, Perkins, and Freeman. They reported no visible movement in the house and the rest of the officers were sent in. Tingles was sure they'd have Christina in custody in a matter of hours. This was his favorite part of being a detective - the results. Investigating and the process of discovering a murderer was satisfying, but there was nothing like finding the son-of-a-bitch and locking them up. Officer Brown had been assigned to translate the hand signals of the officers around the home to Gentry, Tingles, and Johnson so they wouldn't prematurely give themselves away by making too much noise. On the off chance Christina wasn't watching, they didn't want to make themselves known. Brown gave a "perimeter all clear, no motion detected in windows" notice after fifteen minutes or so, followed by a "permission to move in. All officers on stand-by."

"Move in," Gentry replied.

Brown gave the signal to the officers surrounding the home, and within seconds, they'd breached the doors of Brent DeCordts' home. Gentry and Tingles started towards the door of Mrs. DeCordts' home when they heard gunshots coming from down the street. Startled, they turned around and rushed towards Brent DeCordts' home. Gentry yelled into his mouthpiece, "What's going on, Brown?"

"Officer down, officer down!" Brown came back.

"She's going to be reckless now - we have to be careful," Tingles cautioned as they ran towards Brent's home.

They arrived on the lawn, firearms up and pointed in front of them. They slowly approached the door. On the floor, seemingly dead, was Officer Carter. Gentry wondered what the hell he was doing there in the first place - he hadn't been cleared to be back in the field. They saw other officers who had taken refuge behind furniture and doors, one of which motioned towards the stairs. Whoever had shot Carter was up there, presumably Christina. Tingles and Gentry slowly approached the stairs, looking up at the landing to ensure no one waited there for them. In their ears, they heard Brown say, "Suspect detected on second story of the home in front, middle bedroom." Gentry slid in front and motioned for Tingles to follow him without any objection from him. Tingles knew that although Gentry had already been shot once in this investigation, he'd recover quicker than he would himself if he were hit again - provided she didn't get him in the head. Tingles decided they should make themselves known - hell, she knew they were in the house already.

"Christina?" he shouted up the stairs. Gentry shot him a look for "going rogue" again.

Footsteps and thumping were heard from upstairs, followed by muffled screams - Mrs. DeCordts.

"Christina?" Tingles repeated. "Christina, we need to talk! There's no way out of this now. We know you're hurting. We know what the Southerns and the DeCordts did to you."

Gentry and Tingles had started climbing the stairs, slowly making their way up to the second floor as Tingles spoke.

"We know they took away both of your fathers, ostracized your mother, and took away your chances at a happy and successful life. And your mother - she lied to you. That's why you killed her, isn't it? Or was she just collateral damage while you were aiming for us?"

They approached the second-floor landing, still without a word from Christina. They noted the middle room and made their way to it slowly. Tingles faced into the room while Gentry kept an eye on the hallway to ensure she wasn't planning an attack from behind. As they arrived at the doorway, they saw Mrs. DeCordts bound with rope to a chair, her mouth duct-taped shut, eyes wide in fear. The room wasn't a bedroom, but a large office. There was a big cherrywood desk in the center, in front of which sat Mrs. DeCordts. To the right was a seating area with a small couch and two armchairs with a small table in the center, and two side tables on either side of the couch. Antique lamps were placed on the side tables, and a large painting of the DeCordts family was mounted on the wall behind. Every family member's face had been marked through with red paint except Mrs. DeCordts'. Christina had been keeping score.

"Christina?" Tingles said softly.

He heard shuffling and looked into the corner of the room where he saw a figure. The curtains had been drawn almost completely closed, and no lights were on. All they had was the sliver of sunlight coming through the curtains, so he couldn't see the face of the figure and it wasn't speaking. Her silence unnerved him.

"Christina, come on out," Tingles said. "You can't get out of this now. You've killed three people."

"Six, actually," the voice came from behind him.

"Gentry, there's three people in this room," he said calmly. "Not including me."

Gentry turned around, confident now there was no one in the hallway. He saw Tingles looking to the right of the room, so he turned his attention - and his gun - to the left. There stood a tall blonde woman. He couldn't make out her features, but she was definitely the woman in the video footage they'd seen from Gigi's Floral Fabulosity, of which he could be sure. The one thing Gentry hadn't counted on was Christina having a partner. They'd floated the idea that she may, but after determining how personal the murders had been, he'd let it go. Who could it be? Most of the DeCordts were dead, save for Cheryl who sat bound in front of them, and Christina had murdered her only living relative they knew of. Tingles and Gentry stood back-to-back now, each facing an adversary cloaked in darkness. Suddenly the overhead light burst on, dazzling them with light. Gentry's suspicion that the woman in front of him was their suspect was confirmed. From behind him, he heard Tingles begin to speak to the other party in the room.

"Now, now, now. You got me, girl," Tingles said. "I did *not* see this one coming."

"From the brilliant mind of Mister Tingles…." a familiar voice said. "I guess you're not the brilliant detective everyone makes you out to be, are you? I can't have been that difficult to figure out."

"Oh, Kimmie…." Tingles observed.

KIMMIE? Gentry fought the urge to turn around but knew if he did Christina would put a bullet in the back of his head. He'd spotted a Glock in her hand as soon as the lights came up, a remote in the other one - probably to control the lights. They'd learned if Christina loved nothing else, she loved putting on a show.

"This is boring," Christina said. "Just kill 'em and move on."

"Even if you do, there's no way out of this," Gentry responded.

Christina cocked her head and raised the gun she'd kept lowered by her side, a maniacal expression on her face.

Clearly, she hadn't been afraid of them, but she was a woman who'd murdered six people and decapitated at least two. She was a tall, athletic woman which gave Gentry the impression she was a formidable opponent. Their best possible outcome was to bring this standoff to a peaceful conclusion.

"Ha!" Christina half-laughed and half-scoffed at him. "The idea was never to 'get out of this.' The idea was revenge, you simpleton," she snarled, almost yelling.

"For what, exactly?" Gentry asked. "What Tingles said earlier? Something else?"

"Why don't we let Mr. Sissy Pants tell us what he thinks, hm?" she snapped in a sinister tone.

At that moment, he heard a commotion behind him. Tingles made a loud noise as he was rammed into Gentry's back, knocking them both over. Gentry rolled over quickly and saw Kimmie on top of Tingles; she had him on his stomach and was tying his wrists together. He reached for his gun that had fallen on the floor next to him, but before his fingers could reach it, he felt Christina's foot kick his hand with all her strength. He screamed out, and before he could recover himself, he felt her flip him over and begin tying his wrists as well. Gentry and Tingles had been ambushed by Christina and Kimmie. They lured them to Brent's home and were likely planning to kill them along with Mrs. DeCordts. If the two women weren't concerned about not getting arrested, they were more dangerous than ever.

Once Christina and Kimmie had tied their hands, they tied their feet together and slid them on either side of Mrs. DeCordts. The two walked in front of Mrs. DeCordts, Gentry, and Mr. Tingles admiring their work. Mr. Tingles looked closely at Christina; it took him no time before he realized where he recognized her from.

"I'll be damned," he croaked in shock.

"Surprised to see me?" Christina said, kneeling down and looking Mr. Tingles in the eyes. "I kept wondering, every time I saw you, 'When is he going to put it together?' He's such a *brilliant* detective, they say, but he doesn't know he's talking to a serial killer."

Christina giggled and stood upright, beginning to pace.

"Christina, if I'm right you went on a killing spree to exact your revenge against the DeCordts family for taking away the only father you knew. You didn't know Paul was your father until you were an adult, did you? And when you found out - you killed him, too? Because you were angry, he didn't support you and your mother. People have let you down your entire life, haven't they?"

Christina listened, wearing an amused expression but with a hint of surprise. Mr. Tingles knew he was right.

"What I don't know is who killed your father... but you know, don't you? Which DeCordts was it? Brent or Joseph?"

Mrs. DeCordts began mumbling under the duct tape around her mouth. She had something to contribute, but no one could understand her.

"Shut up, bitch!" Kimmie yelled in her ear, but to no avail.

Mrs. DeCordts continued to mumble and scream through the duct tape across her mouth. Kimmie became frustrated with the noise of her moaning and hit her hard on the back of the head. Cheryl's head gave way and fell forward, hanging down, her eyes on the floor. Tingles wasn't sure if she had passed out or if she was dead. Without giving Christina time to respond, he continued:

"Thirty-five years ago, I didn't think it was possible for a twelve-year-old boy to murder a grown man, but I've learned a lot about those boys recently. My money is on Brent. Would you like to know why?"

"By all means, Mr. Tingles…" Christina sneered, with a sinister undertone. "Enlighten us on your theory."

"Brent heard the rumor that his mother was having an affair with Darren Southern - probably from somebody at school. You know how toxic young boys can be at that age. He already had anger issues, so he dealt with the rumor the only way he knew how. Violence. He murdered Darren to punish him for hurting his family and *you saw him do it.*"

Mr. Tingles paused, giving Christina time to respond, but she remained silent. She continued to wear an amused expression.

"After he shot your father in the head, Brent called his mother because he was scared. Mrs. DeCordts came over to your house, helped cover up what her son had done, and left you fatherless. How did I do?"

"Very well Mr. Tingles," Christina acknowledged, smiling chillingly.

She was diabolical. Tingles knew there was no way of reasoning with her.

"You know, my mother was weak," she said. "She could have stood up to the Southerns - for *me*. She made a decision not to. And the DeCordts' - psht! They deserve everything they're getting. Yeah, I killed Paul. HE LEFT ME ALONE WITHOUT A FATHER! I stalked that little bitch of a nurse, shot her in the back of the head - right in her own yard - stole her uniform, and *voila!* I was the new home-health nurse. THIS BITCH…" Christina yelled as she gestured towards Mrs. DeCordts, "…would never have recognized me! None of them had seen me since I was three fucking years old."

Christina was unraveling right in front of them.

"My mother told him she was pregnant, and it was his. He refused to believe her. He deserved to die. And Brent deserved to die for killing the only father I had!"

"What about Joseph?" Tingles asked her. "Did Joseph deserve to die?"

"HE COVERED IT UP!" Christina screamed. "The same fucking reason *this* bitch is going to die." She gestured towards Cheryl, lifted her gun, and fired a shot into Cheryl DeCordts' chest.

Mr. Tingles and Gentry trembled at the sound and the laughter coming from Christina and Kimmie. Christina walked over to Mrs. DeCordts, placing her hand on the victim's wound, and covering her hand in blood. She rushed over to the painting of the DeCordts family on the wall and wiped Cheryl's blood over her face in the painting. She'd done it - murdered them all.

"That's a wrap!" she yelled, turning around to show the room her wide smile.

"It's over now, Christina," Tingles said. "No one else needs to die."

"I'M NOT DONE!" she continued to scream. "This was *your* fault, too, sissy."

Suddenly, two more shots rang through the air....

CHAPTER TWENTY-TWO

As Tingles recovered from the two loud shots, he realized the lights had gone out in the room. It had startled him onto his back, the weight of his body on his hands. He slowly rolled onto his side, taking care not to make a sound and relieving the pressure on his hands and wrists. He heard Kimmie and Christina whispering, questioning where the shot had come from. He thought he could buy some time by staying quiet - maybe they'd think he was dead, struck by the shot. He hoped maybe Gentry had a similar plan. As his eyes adjusted to the darkness, he could see the silhouette of Gentry's body, also lying on its side. He just hoped Gentry hadn't *actually* been shot... again. Tingles listened closely to Kimmie and Christina, noting they were close to the door, probably checking the hallway for the source of the two gunshots. Tingles hadn't heard any glass shattering so they couldn't have come from outside the house. Besides, the curtains didn't leave room for any of the snipers to get a good shot. He thought it could be one of the cops downstairs. Tingles and Gentry had motioned for them to stay where they were, though, so… perhaps not. As his mind made a mental checklist of anyone who may or may not have fired the shots, Tingles felt Mrs. DeCordts' feet brush against him. *She was alive.*

"This is horseshit!" Christina yelled maniacally. "I am sick and fucking tired of playing these childish games."

"Christi…" Kimmie started.

"No!" Christina yelled. Her outburst was followed by a flood of light and the three prisoners were illuminated again.

Tingles tried to play dead, but Christina had seen his face before he closed his eyes. She stomped over to him, cut the tape binding his ankles, and jerked him up on his feet in what seemed like one swift motion.

"C'mon you little shit," she said, standing him in front of her with a gun on his temple. "We're going to find out who's firing shots." Then, talking to someone she couldn't see she said, "Try any funny shit and I'll put a bullet through this sissy's skull. Now come out and play."

There was no response. She carried on talking:

"He was right, you know? About everything. The DeCordts family is full of pieces of shit just like the

Southerns. Every one of 'em deserved what they got. Brent, Joseph, Paul, mama… every single one of them."

Christina had led Tingles into the hallway, walking towards the staircase at the end. Tingles heard Kimmie moving from room to room. He wondered why she hadn't thought to keep an eye on Gentry and Mrs. DeCordts but considered it a stroke of good fortune she hadn't. If Gentry could get out of the tape around his wrists and ankles their plan - or whatever the hell was happening - would be ruined.

"They all left me - abandoned me. I didn't have a family, and no aspirations. Every fucking chance I had in my life was wiped out when Brent murdered my father. And Paul - that piece of shit. *HE LEFT MY MOTHER TO RAISE ME*. No help, not even a goddamn birthday card!"

Christina continued navigating the hallway, one arm wrapped tightly around Tingles' neck, the other pressing her gun firmly on his temple. They stopped at the top of the stairs, feet on the edge of the first step.

"Show yourself or the Lollipop Guild dies!" Christina yelled.

"I know I've put on a few pounds through the years, but I'm not big enough to be a trio – even if they are tiny," Tingles croaked.

"Shut the fuck up!" Christina whispered in his ear, pulling tightly on his neck.

"Only one gonna' die here tonight is you, young lady,

if you don't let him go," a familiar and refreshing voice said. "Now they've already told you there's no way outta' this. Might as well accept it and give yourself up."

"I ain't giving shit up," Christina retorted.

"Tell me something," the voice said. "What's Kimmie Flague got to do with all this?"

"She knows how fucked up this town is. Seems like the only one that does," Christina responded. "She'll make sure this story is told the right way. Somebody needs to tell the world how fucked up the Southerns and the DeCordts' are! She was my eyes... she's how I got to Joseph... and Cheryl."

"You saw 'em every Monday, didn't you?" Tingles asked. "Why couldn't you get them then? Why the theatrics?"

"BECAUSE WHAT'S THE FUCKING FUN IN THAT?" Christina yelled into Tingles' ear. "I wanted to ruin their lives... I wanted them to live in fear of me."

"Let me guess," Tingles started, "...and you would have gotten away with it if it hadn't been for those meddling queers?"

"Y'know, you're both of 'em," the voice said before Christina could become enraged by Tingles' sass. "There's a little of the Southerns *and* the DeCordts in you. But you didn't have to be the worst of 'em. Now you can decide to stop here and make the right decision."

Christina snorted a sinister laugh.

"I am neither of those trash families," she said.

"Tell me, young lady. Did you start working at that flower shop to get closer to Mrs. DeCordts?"

The voice decided to change topics.

"Did your mother know she was the only source for those flowers? The ones Mrs. DeCordts liked? Or did you figure that out on your own?"

"Ha!" Christina shouted. "My mother was a stupid bitch. Too stupid to know anything. That's why she couldn't convince that monster Agatha Southern not to have a paternity test done on me. She ruined *everything*. Her and the DeCordts."

Tingles still hadn't seen the source of the voice - he was hiding somewhere, waiting.

"I know you're angry, Christina," the voice said. "I'd be angry, too. But you've done so much damage already. Hasn't everyone paid for their parts in this now?"

"One more to go!" Christina yelled, pressing her gun further into Tingles' temple.

"You meant for me to be called into this, didn't you?" Tingles croaked. "I was the last on your list to exact your revenge, wasn't I?"

"The last to go... has seen the first six go before him..." Christina hissed, mockingly.

"No one else needs to die, Christina," the voice said.

"Oh, I think he does," she responded calmly, followed by another loud shot.

Tingles found himself rolling down the flight of stairs until finding the first landing. Another body hit him, followed by several moments of quiet and throbbing pain. Tingles heard Kimmie yell indistinguishably from upstairs. They'd all been in the house together for hours and the sun had set. There was a sliver of light coming from the upstairs bedroom, but otherwise, they were in pitch blackness again.

Tingles listened for voices from downstairs but heard nothing. Suddenly he felt Christina moving. He was weak from the fall and being tied up, but he knew if she got a hold of him again, she'd kill him. He could tell from the little bit of light available his feet were facing her stomach. He managed himself into the fetal position, knees to his chest, and kicked them out as fast and hard as he could, kicking Christina in the stomach. She yelled out in pain and Tingles threw himself down the second flight of stairs. As he landed, he heard Christina getting to her feet, grunting in pain and anger.

"I'll fucking kill you, Tingles!" she screamed out. She raised her gun at him at the bottom of the stairs and cocked it.

"Over my dead body," the omnipresent voice said loudly and confidently. Officer Johnson stepped around the corner from the downstairs hallway, Glock pointed upward at Christina and fired off two shots, hitting her directly in the chest.

Christina looked astounded as the bullets lodged in her body. She fell forward, slamming into the landing like a bag of potatoes. Johnson slowly made his way up the stairs and nudged her with his foot. When he was sure she was at least unconscious, he leaned down and took her pulse. Satisfied she was dead he made his way back down the stairs and untied Mr. Tingles.

"You alright? You took a helluva fall."

"I'm fine, I'm fine," Tingles said, as Johnson started to get up. Tingles grabbed his arm as to ask him to stay.

"There's one more bitch to take down," he said. He began to stand, turned back and balanced on his knee as he lifted Tingles up to sit upright. He placed a hand on Tingles' cheek and said, "Would it be alright if I kissed you?"

"Just like a man," Tingles said. "Surrounded by dead bodies and all he can think of is his libido."

"You're right," Johnson agreed and started to rise again.

Tingles grabbed and pulled him back towards him.

"I didn't say no," the two men shared a passionate kiss that ended with Tingles pushing him away. "Now go get that trash and bring my friend back safely."

Johnson got up and ran up the stairs, leaping over Christina's body. Tingles was impressed with his ability to move so well at his age, and if his stamina was as good as that kiss, he couldn't wait to see more.

Johnson reached the top of the stairs carefully, pulling out his flashlight and slowly making his way around the corner towards the bedrooms.

"Kimmie?" he said. His voice was calm. "Kimmie, Christina is dead. It's over."

He heard muffled moaning from the center bedroom. Making his way into the room his flashlight revealed Gentry, unconscious on the floor, and Mrs. DeCordts struggling to release herself from the rope and duct tape binding her. She'd lost a lot of blood, and Johnson was shocked she had the strength to continue trying to free herself. Johnson checked Gentry's pulse - light, but it was there, and he noticed a wound on his head. Mrs. DeCordts began screaming through the duct tape on her mouth. Johnson slowly removed it, trying to avoid ripping her hair out.

"She's gone," Mrs. DeCordts managed to get out as Johnson finally peeled the tape from her mouth.

"How do you know?" Johnson asked.

"There's a door through the closet that leads downstairs and into the basement. It leads to my house."

"Son of a bitch!" Johnson said. He called through his walkie to the other officers to inform them Kimmie had escaped and was likely at Mrs. DeCordts' home, then called for medics to help her, Tingles and Gentry.

While he waited for medics, Johnson walked back down the stairs to Tingles who had propped himself on the wall in the hallway. He kneeled down, took Tingles' cheeks in both palms and planted his lips on Tingles' again. Tingles grabbed both of Johnson's wrists and held onto him, every nerve in his body electrified by the tall, handsome hunk's soft lips against his. When Johnson finally moved his lips away, Tingles saw tears filling his eyes.

"Am I that bad of a kisser?" Tingles joked, winking at Johnson.

"This was the second time I thought I'd lost you before getting to say…"

"Say?" Tingles questioned after several long seconds.

"I think I love you, Tingles."

Mr. Tingles allowed Johnson's declaration of love to sink in; it was a feeling he hadn't known in over a decade. He felt himself coming alive despite having been tackled, tied up, and thrown down two flights of stairs. At sixty-three years old, Tingles thought he may have finally found his knight in shining armor.

"Officer Johnson," Tingles said. "I think I love you, too."

CHAPTER TWENTY-THREE

As the sun began to rise the following morning, the streets were ablaze with emergency vehicle lights and caution tape blocking the road. Mr. Tingles lay on a stretcher, Johnson's hand tightly clasped around his own. Gentry, having finally been untied and his head wound patched up, was still inside, barking orders at the officers after refusing any more medical attention. Mrs. DeCordts had been rushed to the hospital with a police escort - she'd be arrested for her role in covering up Darren Southern's murder.

Mr. Tingles regretted not solving the case before everyone else had died, but at least one responsible party would be held accountable. Kimmie hadn't been found. She was on the run and Tingles had a feeling they hadn't heard the last of her.

Tingles looked up at the sky in silence, the soft southern breeze grazing his skin, and the feeling of peace Johnson's hand gave him. In a few short weeks his life had changed tremendously. He'd come out of retirement, solved a thirty-five-year-old murder case, made new friends, and fallen in love. To think he'd been such a recluse before all this seemed laughable. He'd been reminded his age was no reason to "settle down." He was still good at what he did and loved doing it. The satisfaction he gleaned from catching criminals was unparalleled, and he'd decided - right there on that stretcher - there was nothing else he wanted to do with the rest of his life (except for maybe Johnson). Besides, now there were only *two* unsolved murders from his entire career. If he'd been able to solve the Southern murder, he knew he could solve the other two. Especially if he enlisted the help of Gentry and Johnson.

As Tingles lay on the stretcher thinking, Gentry approached and informed them they'd be wrapping up soon. He sternly told the emergency responder to get Tingles to the hospital and smiled as he noticed his hand in Johnson's. Gentry felt a sense of relief, himself. The most difficult case of his short career was over, and they'd solved it. He felt very proud. Though he couldn't take full credit for their solving the case, he was an instrumental part of their success, and he knew it. He'd done what he set out to do and proven himself as a good detective. He was suddenly craving more cases like this, knowing that little ole' Reidsville couldn't possibly give him the thrill he was seeking. As he began to walk away, he heard Tingles' voice call him.

"I had a thought," he said, wincing from the pain of falling down two flights of stairs.

"Oh yeah? I'm not surprised," Gentry responded, grinning. "You can rest, Tingles, we solved it." He looked from Tingles to Johnson adding, "All of us."

"Not about the case, you buffoon," Tingles said, chuckling through the pain. "I think we - all three of us - should start a private investigator firm for ourselves. We make an awfully good team."

"Hmm," Johnson mused. "We do make a great team."

"Yeah. We sure do, but..." Gentry started.

"No buts!" Tingles said encouragingly. "Young man, if I've learned anything these past several weeks it's that life doesn't stop because you're scared, or getting older, or whatever. Time will keep right on ticking, and you can either do what makes you happy or get left in the dust."

Gentry looked at Tingles for a few moments and his entire life flashed before his eyes. Not in that, "death is upon me" way, but in a peaceful, coming-to-terms way. Gentry had accomplished something in the past few weeks he never thought he'd accomplish. He had started building a life for himself he never thought was possible. This case had given him a chance to prove to himself and the townspeople that he was capable of being a great detective. More importantly he had proven that to his parents. He didn't have to stay in Reidsville if he didn't want to because there was nothing left there for him but disappointment and bad memories.

"What d'ya think, Johnson?" he finally said.

"I think we *do* make a helluva team," Johnson replied.

"So, what are we? The Pointer Sisters?" Gentry joked, smiling.

"More like The Chicks, don't you think?" Johnson said.

"Boys, boys…" Tingles said. "We're clearly The Andrews Sisters. And, um…" he added, looking directly at Gentry, "…you don't know Bette Davis, but you know the Pointer Sisters?"

"I'm not a complete lost cause," Gentry answered, laughing.

The trio continued to banter for several minutes about which famous female trio they were until Tingles raised a hand to silence them.

"Gentlemen, whichever girl band we are, we are first and foremost great detectives. Here and now I officially declare Detectives Tingles, Gentry, and Johnson hereby form Tingles & Associates Private Investigators Firm. Let's go save the world from one straight criminal at a time."

Epilogue

Kimmie Flague rushed through Raleigh Union Station, a ticket to Pennsylvania in hand. It wouldn't be her last stop, but it would get her far enough away from Reidsville, North Carolina to get a plan together. She'd prepared to go into hiding from the beginning. She'd written Christina's story as it happened; she planned to finish it - including her escape - then send it to a publisher. She didn't care about the money. In fact, she'd send the manuscript to publishers with a letter relinquishing her rights to any copyrights, royalties, or even credit. All she wanted was fame and she'd have it – even without formally receiving the credit. The fact she'd been the accomplice to a serial killer - submitting a manuscript with a front row seat to the murder of six people, while she herself was running from the authorities, would make for an instant bestseller. That's all Kimmie dreamed of.

Christina had found Kimmie poking around the investigation early on. Kimmie knew Christina didn't care about her, she only wanted someone to tell her story. Kimmie was so desperate that when Christina approached her and said, "I think I have an offer you can't refuse," she didn't refuse it – even though it meant being an accomplice to murder. One thing Kimmie and Christina had in common was they came from broken families. So, when given the opportunity to make a name for herself, Kimmie took it with the understanding that she wouldn't willingly die for the cause.

When Christina had led Mr. Tingles downstairs, she took the opportunity to run. They had been partners, but Christina didn't care if she lived or died and Kimmie did. Her relationship with Cheryl made her aware of the secret doors in hers and Brent's homes and the tunnel that connected them. She knew it took exactly ten minutes to run from one home to the other once she got to it, and approximately three minutes from the second floor to the tunnel. All in all, she needed about fifteen minutes to escape to Cheryl's home and a few extra to sneak out into the woods behind Cheryl's. Since everyone was more concerned about catching Christina, she had the perfect opportunity and it worked. She got away, she'd written the perfect account of a serial killer, and Mr. Tingles and his team would never catch her.

She finally boarded the train, found her way to her

car, and got settled. Once the train started towards Pennsylvania Kimmie pulled out a notebook and ball-point pen to write:

Mr. Tingles,

I know you'll be tempted to try and find me - don't. Not that it matters, but I didn't kill any of those people, anyway. It was all Christina. I promised to tell her story and she paid me well to do it. Her story - our story - will be one of a kind. No doubt you'll write your own telling of the events, so I'm sure you understand.
We'll meet again someday, but in the meantime… I hope you think of me every time you see Evita.
All my love,
Kimmie
P.S. Tell Isaiah I said hello.

About the Author

Sean is a 37-year-old husband, cat and puppy dad, student, social justice advocate, and lover of words. He is earning his Master of Arts in Sociology, specializing in Queer culture, and using his voice to write queer characters that show the beauty, value, and vibrancy. He has been deeply influenced by writers such as Agatha Christie, Sir Arthur Conan Doyle, Stephen Spotswood, and A.C. Rosen. A huge fan of mystery, thrillers, horror films, and television, he finds inspiration from Criminal Minds, Scream, and Only Murders in the Building. He hopes to create captivating and mysterious stories such as those that have influenced him - only make it gay!

Follow the Author

www.patreon.com/Seandroachauthor

Insta: @socionerd88

BlueSky: socionerd.bsky.social

Also Available from Gold Dust Publishing

- <u>The House on Dead Man's Curve</u>
  By J. S. Roach

- <u>Until Death: An Eric Kent Investigation</u>
  By Rey Nichols

- <u>Reflections</u> – Our charity book featuring over 40 authors contributing. (including J.S. Roach)

- <u>The Purple Menace and the Tobacco Prince</u>
  By Wade Beauchamp

- <u>The Sword's Secret: Ancient Wonders – Book 1</u>
  By Chris Cole

- <u>The Vampire Crusades: The Acquisition – Book 1</u>
  By J.S. Roach

www.ingramcontent.com/pod-product-compliance
Lightning Source LLC
Chambersburg PA
CBHW020753310726
48969CB00002B/517